Tate Harrison **a** ...
man to figure o...

One minute he was out boozing with Overo's
hell-raisers, and the next he was bringing her baby
daughter into the world with as much tender concern
as she might have expected from her child's own
father. She'd never seen Tate more shaken, nor more
jubilant. She didn't know what to make of it all.

Still, Amy breathed a long, gratified sigh. She
had had to trust Tate with a most intimate and
momentous task, and he had come through for her
in spades.

But she wasn't going to start relying on him, she
reminded herself. The man's feet were made of sand.

Still, he had more heart than she'd ever given him
credit for. She wouldn't *depend* on that particular
muscle, but until she could get back on her feet
again, it wouldn't hurt to lean on it, just a little....

Dear Reader,

Welcome to Silhouette *Special Edition* . . . welcome to romance.

Last year I requested your opinions on the books that we publish. Thank you for the many thoughtful comments. For the next couple of months, I'd like to share quotes with you from those letters. This seems very appropriate while we are in the midst of our THAT SPECIAL WOMAN! promotion. Each one of our readers is a very *special* woman, as heroic as the heroines in our books.

This month, our THAT SPECIAL WOMAN! is Kelley McCormick, a woman who takes the trip of a lifetime and meets the man of her dreams. You'll meet Kelley and her Prince Charming in *Grand Prize Winner!* by Tracy Sinclair.

Also in store for you this month is *The Way of a Man*, the third book in Laurie Paige's WILD RIVER TRILOGY. And not to be missed are terrific books from other favorite authors—Kathleen Eagle, Pamela Toth, Victoria Pade and Judith Bowen.

I hope you enjoy this book, and all of the stories to come!

Sincerely,

Tara Gavin
Senior Editor

QUOTE OF THE MONTH:

"I enjoy characters I can relate to—female characters who are wonderful people packaged in very ordinary coverings and men who see beyond looks and who are willing to work at a relationship. I enjoy stories of couples who stick with each other and work through difficult times. Thank you, Special Edition, for the many, many hours of enjoyment."

—M. Greenleaf, Maryland

KATHLEEN EAGLE

BROOMSTICK COWBOY

Silhouette®

SPECIAL EDITION®

Published by Silhouette Books

America's Publisher of Contemporary Romance

For Judy Baer, Sandy Huseby and Pamela Bauer, on
our tenth anniversary.

Vive Prairie Writers' Guild!

 SILHOUETTE BOOKS

ISBN 0-373-09848-0

BROOMSTICK COWBOY

Copyright © 1993 by Kathleen Eagle

This edition published by arrangement with Harlequin Enterprises B. V.

® and TM are trademarks of Harlequin Enterprises B. V., used under
license. Trademarks indicated with ® are registered in the United States
Patent and Trademark Office, the Canadian Trade Marks Office and in
other countries.

Printed in U.S.A.

KATHLEEN EAGLE

is a transplant from New England to Minnesota, where she and her husband, Clyde, make their home with two of their three children. She's considered writing to be her "best talent" since she was about nine years old, and English and history were her "best subjects." After fourteen years of teaching high school students about writing, she saw her own first novel in print in 1984. Since then, she's published many more novels with Silhouette Books and Harlequin Historicals that have become favorites for readers worldwide. She also writes mainstream novels and has received awards from the Romance Writers of America, *Romantic Times* and *Affaire de Coeur*.

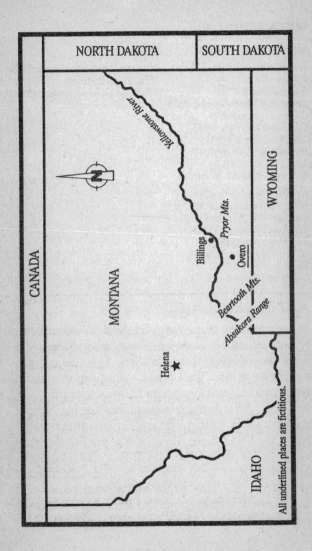

Prologue

Tate Harrison cupped his big, callused hands around his face and peeked through the back door window into the Beckers' kitchen. Except for the two plates standing in the dish drainer along with two forks and a pair of tall tumblers, turned bottoms up, the place was as neat and tidy as the rows in a Kansas cornfield. It was Amy's kitchen, so naturally it would be. The only fingerprints would be those he was making on the glass right now, pressing his face to the window. The floor looked so clean he could almost smell the pine soap, and the stainless-steel sink was flooded with Indian summer sunshine, pouring through the ruffles of a yellow gingham curtain.

He shoved his hands in his jacket pockets and gave the rambler-style farmhouse a cursory inspection on the outside. The yellow trim was in pretty good shape, but the white clapboard siding sure needed a coat of paint. White sheers hung in the side window, but he would bet there were yellow curtains down the hall. Yellow was Amy's color. It looked great with her dark hair and dark eyes. Black-Eyed Susan, he'd called her, but that had been a long time ago.

He rapped on the glass a second time, put his hands back up and peered again. As always, Tate was on the outside looking in. He liked it that way, especially whenever he came home to Overo. The best part of Montana was definitely the outside. Plenty of elbow room. Plenty of scenery. Plenty of opportunity for a cowboy to move on to greener pastures whenever he felt like it. Moving on had become his stock in trade, taking him out of state, even out of the country, but whenever he was in town—and it had been a while— he always looked in on the Beckers.

He'd had mixed feelings this time about paying his more-or-less regular call. Up until a year ago Kenny Becker had been leasing the land Tate had inherited after his stepfather died. He felt a little funny about showing up now to talk business. Kenny was Tate's best friend, and Tate wanted to sell him the land eventually, whenever Kenny could swing the financing. At least, that had always been the plan.

When Kenny had dropped the lease last year, the only explanation had come in a note that said they were "cutting back on the horses." Kenny had assured him that there were plenty of neighbors interested in picking up the lease. But Tate wasn't interested in leasing his land to anyone else. He had called to wish the family a merry Christmas and to tell Kenny to go ahead and use the land, cut the hay on shares. He'd asked only a token percentage for himself, because he knew what Amy would say if she thought he was giving them something for nothing. But he and Kenny were friends, and if times were tough, he wanted to help out. He'd managed to keep his own financial obligations to a minimum.

"You sure you guys are okay?" Tate had asked over the phone. He couldn't imagine Kenny cutting his horse herd. He loved every useless broomtail he kept around the place, and year after year that sentiment had helped him run his operation into the red. But that was Kenny. "You know, if you need to, you can sell my share of the hay and use the cash to—"

"Hey, thanks, buddy, but we're doin' just fine. Amy's got us into this sideline that's...well, it's a long story, but next year things'll start lookin' up. You oughta get married and settle down, Tate. I tell you..."

"I'm doin' fine, too, Ken," Tate had said. "Come fall, we'll take a look at where things stand. If you want to pick up the lease again, fine. If you don't think you're gonna want to buy it like we planned, I'll probably just unload it. My banker tells me the mineral rights are worth more now than the grass."

Lately Tate had been thinking he wouldn't mind selling the land and cutting the last of his ties. He'd left Overo when his stepfather died seven years ago, and hadn't been back in at least the last two, maybe longer. There were a thousand other places where he could be outside without feeling quite so much like an *outsider.* He shouldn't be feeling that way anymore, not when he was standing here on the back step of a house he'd spent as much time in as his own when he was growing up. Kenny Becker was his *best friend.* Always had been.

But Amy was his best friend's wife. And they'd never made a very good threesome.

Damn, he'd knocked three times now, and nothing seemed to be moving except a fat calico cat. She padded across the white linoleum, stopped by the back door and blinked a couple of times, then rounded the corner and ambled down the basement steps. It all made for a pretty disappointing homecoming. Tate had been looking forward to surprising them, earning a couple of smiles, maybe even a couple of hugs and a home-cooked meal. He tried to remember whether he'd still had his beard the last time he'd been back. They might not even recognize him since he'd started shaving regularly again. Well, fairly regularly. No, Kenny would, he amended. Fifty years from now, when they were both nearsighted ol' codgers, Ken would still know him right off.

Amy was another story. She wasn't interested in knowing Tate Harrison. She had no use for his good intentions or his excuses or his apologies. She tolerated him because she loved Kenny. He wasn't sure she was really interested in knowing Kenny, either, not the same Kenny he knew. But she loved him just as sure as she had no use for his best friend.

A mystery, that woman. The kind you could stay up all night reading and never figure out until you hit the very last page. She was a city girl turned country. One minute she could be as stiff-necked as an old school-marm, the next she'd be bubbling over like she'd just popped her cork. Smart and sexy both. Tate figured she'd outsmarted herself when she'd married Ken, thinking all she had to do to shape him up was change the company he kept. On her wedding day, Tate had sincerely wished her luck. From the looks of things, somebody's luck was stretched a little thin right about now.

Tate tried the door, but it was locked. That had to mean they'd gone into town together. Kenny never locked the door, because he never had a key. If there'd been anybody out in the barn, they would have peeked out when they heard the pickup, but just to make sure, Tate walked around back and gave a holler. The only response came from the two dogs that had been yap-pin' to beat hell when he drove up. A Border collie and a Catahoula Leopard, both trying to see who could jump the highest inside the chain-link kennel. Tate didn't remember the kennel being there, next to the clothesline. The dogs were new, too. He wondered what had happened to the old black Lab he and Kenny used to take with them when they'd go fishing.

On the way to his pickup he turned the corner around the dilapidated yard fence and nearly tripped over a pint-size red-and-white bicycle lying on its side in the gravel. Their little boy couldn't be old enough to ride a bike. Last time Tate had seen the little squirt he'd barely been toddling around, pigeon-toed like his ol' man. His hair was curly like Kenny's, too, only lighter, but he had his mother's big brown eyes. Cute little tyke. Cute enough to make a guy think he might want one of his own someday.

Tate lit a cigarette and leaned his backside against the headlight of his pickup. The crisp October breeze felt good against his face. This was a pretty spot. Plenty of water and grass, and a fine view of the snow-capped mountains. Wouldn't be long before the lowlands would snuggle under a blanket of snow and sleep until springtime. The only time he ever got homesick was when he thought of the Becker place. He'd sold his own house right off the foundation, along with the pole barns, the grain bins, even the damn toolshed. All he'd kept was the land. If you wanted to make a go of it on the land, you had to sacrifice, and you never knew what kind of forfeiture the land might demand. It had taken all it would ever get from Tate. He'd been making a damn good living as a rodeo cowboy, truck driver, construction worker—whatever came along. He'd socked the lease payments away in the bank. He didn't need the land, and it damn sure wasn't claiming his best years.

Didn't look like it was claiming much of the sweat off ol' Kenny's brow, either. He hadn't brought in much hay. The half section west of the house hadn't been cut. Worse yet, somebody's mangy sheep were grazing on it. Just like Kenny to let a neighbor take advantage of his good nature. But from the looks of things, Kenny couldn't afford to be so damned good-natured. Other than the dogs and the trespassing sheep, Tate didn't see too many signs of life around the place. No horses in the corral out back. Not a cow in sight.

The more he thought about it, the less he liked what he was seeing. Tate dropped his cigarette on the gravel driveway and ground it under his boot heel. Fishing in his jacket for his keys, he jerked the pickup door open. Surely on his way to town he would see a supply of square bales, stacked up in a nice long wall close to the road, where it wouldn't be too hard to reach in the winter. Probably down on his land, near the old homesite, where the access would still be pretty good. Maybe on the alfalfa field, where Kenny should have been able to get a good two cuttings this year. He should have hauled the bales in closer, though, damn his lazy hide.

But, then, that was Kenny.

Chapter One

"What do you mean, *ever since Kenny Becker kicked the bucket?*"

Tate was ready to pop bartender Ted Staples in the mouth for coming up with such a sick joke. But Ted wasn't smiling. In fact, Ted had stopped pouring drinks. He set the bottle of Jack Daniel's down on the bar as if it were a delicate piece of crystal, and he looked at Tate with about as much surprise as ever registered on the gaunt man's leathery face.

"I mean, ever since Kenny *died,*" Ted said more carefully this time. "Is that better? Since Kenny died, the women around here have been drivin' me crazy with phone calls, checkin' up on their men."

"Checking up..." The hinges in Tate's jaw went rusty on him. He could even taste the rust in the back of his mouth. No, the word *died* wasn't any better. For an instant the letters on the neon Pabst sign above the bar swelled up and blurred clean out of focus. Hell, he was only on his first drink, and somehow he'd missed the part where he'd taken a boot in the gut. "What in hell are you talkin' about, Ted?"

"I usually tell 'em the man ain't here or he just left, but you hear that damn he's-been-gone-too-long tone in their voice, kinda scared and trembly, and you know what they're worried about."

"Kenny..."

"Well, you know—" Since they'd hit on a touchy subject, Ted splashed another shot in Tate's glass for good measure. "—it took us a while to find him. Surprised you didn't come back for the funeral, Tate. You two used to be close enough to use the same toothpick. Where you saw one, you saw the other."

"When..." It felt as though somebody had just pulled the walls in a few feet. Tate was suddenly short on air and voice. It took a long pull on his drink to sear the goop out of his pipes. He pressed his lips together and pushed his big black Stetson back so he could get a better look at Ted's face. He needed to make damn sure the old man wasn't putting him on. "When?"

"Why, late last winter." Ted turned to Gene Leslie, who occupied the bar stool on the inside corner. "Was it March?"

"Early March." Gene swept his quilted jacket back with arms akimbo, poking his gut out while he took a moment to puzzle all this out.

Tate was listening, waiting for some sense to be made here. He felt clammy under the back of his shirt, under his hatband. He wanted to shed his jacket, open the door, let some air in the place. But nobody took his jacket off in the Jackalope Bar, because there was no place to put it, and everybody wore a cowboy hat, because you didn't hang out at the Jackalope unless you were a cowboy.

"Take that back," Gene amended contemplatively. "Believe it might've been closer to the middle of the month. Them heifers started calving on the tenth, and I believe..." He squinted, focusing on Tate through a haze of blue smoke. "You didn't know about Kenny?"

Tate shook his head, trying to clear it of the flak and home in on some answers. "Know what? What the hell happened?"

"He was here that day." Ted wiped his hand on the white towel he'd tucked into the front of his belt for an apron, then wagged his finger at the center booth next to the far wall. Two cowboys looked up briefly, then went back to nursing their brews and puffing their smokes as soon as they realized the finger wasn't pointed at them. "Sittin' right over there at that table, horse tradin' with Ticker Thomas 'til late afternoon, early evening. When his wife called, I told her Kenny'd left before suppertime, and I thought sure he was sober."

"Turned out he was, which was too bad," Gene added. "He'd 'a had more alcohol in him, he'd 'a made it through the night. My uncle Amos lived for two days in the middle of November when he went in the ditch that time over by Roundup.''

"Your uncle Amos is too ugly to live and too or- nery to die," thick-tongued Charlie Dennison said. The story was coming at Tate from all sides now, with Charlie getting into it from his perch near the door.

"You're damn straight. He was tanked up pretty good and glad of it, even when they cut off his frost- bit toes." Gene adjusted his hat in a gesture that al- lowed no two ways about the facts in either story. "Poor ol' Kenny should'a had a few more shots un- der his belt."

"Kenny only drank beer," Tate said. "I didn't see his old Ford pickup out at his place. Was it a—"

Gene shook his head. "Nah, he didn't wreck his pickup. He got throwed. Ground was still froze hard as rock. Split his head open like a melon."

"Nobody's figured out yet what he was doin' out ridin' that horse that time of night," Ted put in. "Like I said, his ol' lady'd been callin' around to hell and back. Then she went out lookin' for him, so there was nobody home. He must'a drove his pickup out in the pasture, caught a horse and went off ridin' bareback, far as anybody can tell. Damnedest thing."

"Moon was bright as hell that night, and it was cold as a witch's tit," Charlie recalled.

"We used to go out together on nights like that," Tate said. He could picture the moonlight flooding the snow-covered hillsides. Kenny loved those nights, when the big black velvet sky was filled with stars and their voices cracked the cold hush with pithy adoles- cent wisdom. "Bareback, too, so you'd keep your butt warm. Twice as warm as a woman and half the trouble," he remembered with a melancholy smile.

"Women don't usually buck as hard," Gene said.

"Tell you what, Leslie," Charlie grumbled. "Any woman does any buckin' with *you* has got be three ax handles wide in the hip and horse-faced as hell," Charlie said.

Ted let the perpetual banter go in one ear and out the other, but Tate's difficulty drew rare concern. "They must not've been able to track you down, Tate."

"Maybe they didn't try." Amy, he thought. Maybe Amy hadn't wanted him around when she'd buried her husband.

"That little girl was pretty damn broke up, but I'd be willing to bet she tried to call you or something."

Tate wasn't going to argue. "Who found him?"

"She did."

"Amy?"

"The pickup wasn't back, see, so that kinda throwed 'em off for a while. But when they found Kenny's pickup, and then they found the horse still wearin' a hackamore, well, they sent out a helicopter. A bunch of us went out on horseback. But his wife took those dogs of hers, and she went out on foot. She found him."

"He'd slid down into a ravine. Don't know what all he ran into. Head split open like a damn melon." Gene was stuck on the melon image.

It was all a dream. A bad one. The kind that wouldn't go away when he woke up. Tate knew it well;

he'd had it before. He cast his gaze at the sooty ceiling and whispered, "Jesus."

Jesus, get me out of here.

Jesus, make it not be true.

Jesus, give him back.

He sighed heavily and dug into his shirt pocket for a cigarette. "Hope she got a decent price for her stock."

"She ain't sold much yet," Ted reported. "She says she's gonna run the place herself, her and the boy."

Tate glanced up from the match he'd struck on his thumbnail. "The kid's only, what? Three or four?"

"Hell, I was feedin' stock when I was four years old," Charlie claimed.

Gene laughed. "The hell you were, Dennison. Even at *forty*-four you wouldn't know which end to feed."

Tate dragged deeply on his cigarette, hoping the smoke would do better than whiskey at calming his innards. One of the cowboys had gotten up from the booth and chucked some change into the jukebox. It rattled its way down the hollow tube and clunked when it hit bottom. If they'd pitched it down Tate's throat, it would have made the same damn sound.

"She hired any help?" he asked. The cowboy punched his numbers, and up came the steel guitars.

"Well, she tried," Ted said. "She run one scarecrow-lookin' guy off with a shotgun after about a week last summer. Said he'd tried to make a pass at her."

"My uncle Amos used to say some widows are just like cask-aged wine, and some are pure vinegar," Gene said.

"Your uncle Amos oughta take another drive out to Roundup," Charlie said. He was listening to Ted's story with increasing interest. "None of her family came to help her out? You woulda thought..."

"Her mother lives in Florida somewhere. She was here for a little while after Kenny died, but she went back." In response to Gene's signal, Ted slid another bottle of Blue Ribbon his way. "Mrs. Becker's got spunk—I'll say that for her. Winter's a bad time to sell, anyway. If she can hold out a few months, I'd say she'll get a good price for the place."

"She's over to the sale barn now," Charlie said. "I was just there. Looks like she's gonna run some horses through."

"Horseflesh is goin' pretty cheap," Gene said as he raised the bottle to his thin lips.

Tate was tempted to stay right where he was and get himself blind drunk, fight absurdity with absurdity. These people were talking about Kenny like it made perfect sense that he was dead. Like it was not possible for Kenny to be the next man to park his old green pickup out front. Like the next guy that flung that creaky front door open and let in a blast of cold air couldn't be Kenny.

It couldn't be true. It was inconceivable that Tate couldn't come home to Overo and buy Kenny a drink, listen to his tall tales and hear that bizarre, high-pitched laugh of his. Kenny was only thirty years old, for God's sake. He couldn't be lying stone cold and silent in a box six feet deep in the ground. That was the meaning of *dead*. His best friend couldn't really be dead.

Blind drunk was one thing, but Tate didn't know if he could pull off a *deaf* drunk, and he didn't think he could handle any more of Hank Williams' "Cold Cold Heart" without getting awkwardly choked up. He tossed the rest of his drink down and stubbed his cigarette in the plastic ashtray. After he slid off the stool he slapped a twenty on the bar.

Ted pushed the cash back across the polished wood. "It's on the house, Tate. I'm real sorry you had to find out this way."

"Good a way as any," Tate answered as he backed away from the bar. "You give these guys another round on me. For Kenny. There were no flowers at his funeral with my name on 'em, so—" his gesture was all-inclusive "—you guys remember Kenny kindly over the next round. He always gave the best he had."

The words tasted a little saccharine in Tate's mouth, but everybody readily agreed with his assessment. Hell, yes, drink up, boys; Kenny Becker was a damn good friend.

"You say she's over at the sale barn?" Out of habit he flipped up the collar of his sheepskin jacket, even though he left it hanging open in front.

"Last I saw."

"Think I'll pay my respects."

Tate didn't feel like pretending to be glad to see people, but it was like old home week the minute he walked into the Overo Livestock Auction. Not too many of his own friends, but several of his stepdad's old cronies recognized him and made a fuss over seeing his picture in *Rodeo Sports News*. It was no big deal, he told them. He'd made a few good rides this summer, but he hadn't made the National Finals yet.

Bill Walker insisted that Tate had "done real good" and his ol' man would be proud of him. To this day Tate couldn't think of Oakie Bain as *his ol' man,* even though he knew his real father only from pictures. But it would have been rude to take exception to the claim aloud. And something in the back of his mind regularly put the skids to downright rudeness.

He stepped around the boxes of baby rabbits and mewling kittens the country kids had for sale near the front door and shook hands with longtime neighbor Myron Olson. Myron wouldn't let go until he'd figured out how long it had been, so Tate had to guess six or seven years before he could slap the old man on the back and head up the steps to the gallery. He didn't look for a seat. Instead he lit a cigarette and leaned against a post near the doorway, where he could observe without being seen.

It didn't take long to spot her. He couldn't see much more than the top of her head, which stood out from all the cowboy hats and straw-hued mops like a fur coat in a dime store. Her hair was the color of a dark bay mare he'd had when he was a kid. You could only see the red tones when she stood out in the sun. Indoors, it was a rich shade of ranch mink. She'd kept it long. Today she had it done up in a braided ponytail. She was sitting way over to the side, down close to the activity, but the crowd was pretty sparse. She was all alone.

She seemed intent on the proceedings in the ring, but maybe she was staring hard because her thoughts were somewhere else. He wondered where. She looked like a high school girl, sitting in class and paying close attention to the teacher. Could have been a foreign language class the way the auctioneer was rattling off numbers a mile a minute. No problem for Amy. He hadn't known her when she was in school, but she was the type who had probably aced every class. Poor Kenny had nearly bombed out, but Tate had loaned him enough of his homework to see Kenny through to graduation.

He wondered if she knew that. She'd pegged Tate for a troublemaker. He'd always been the one getting poor ol' Kenny into hot water. He wondered if she knew he'd also gotten Kenny through school. Didn't matter, Tate told himself. By and large, she had his number.

He watched the numbers flash on the electronic sign. Good saddle horses were going for killer prices. He took a long slow drag on his cigarette as he listened to the auctioneer describe the merits of the next lot. Chief among them, the next four horses had belonged to the late Kenny Becker, who'd raised some of the best quarter horses in the state. According to reliable reports, these were the best of his herd.

Tate figured that auctioneer Cal Swick was likely stretching the truth pretty thin. These were probably the only ones Kenny'd ever managed to break out, despite all his big-scale horse-breeding plans. Kenny was a dreamer, but maybe Cal believed the reliable reports himself.

Saddle horses always sold better if somebody showed them under saddle, so Tate was glad to see that

Amy had hired one of the kids who hung around the stock pens to ride her horses through for her. He remembered when he and Kenny used to compete for the same kind of job. They'd bet each other who could get his Saturday chores done first and beat the other one to the sale barn for the chance to earn a few bucks. People usually picked Tate over Kenny if they needed a rider. He'd been born looking the part.

The bidding wasn't going anywhere, so Tate decided to jump in and run the sorrel gelding up a few dollars. He pushed his hat back, gave a subtle nod and a hand signal, skipping over a few increments to make people take a second look. It worked the first time around, but by the time all four horses had gone through, the buyers had dropped the bid on him twice. He was satisfied. Five hundred was a damn good batting average. The only catch would be settling up in the sales office without letting Amy catch him. Then he would go out to the pens and figure out what to do with two horses he didn't need.

He'd bought himself a bald-faced sorrel mare and a buckskin gelding. A five- and a six-year-old, from the looks of their teeth. Well fed, sound legs. He was checking the buckskin's hooves when the woman of the hour caught him red-handed.

"You paid way too much for that one."

Her voice always got to him. Smooth and low for a woman's, it had a seductively smoky quality. He glanced up and connected immediately with earth-mother eyes peering at him between the fence rails. He straightened slowly.

"Hello, Amy."

"It's not like you to wait until after you've paid your money to inspect the goods, Tate Harrison. That was always one of the differences between you and Ken."

"I got here late." He brushed his hands off on his denim-covered thighs, choosing to take the remark the way he took his whiskey. Perfectly straight. "But I can usually spot a good saddle horse in the ring pretty easy."

"So I've heard. Ken swore by your horse sense." She spoke the name so easily that she nearly put him at ease, too. But then she added, "Unfortunately, you took it with you when you left."

He half expected her to take the high ground by climbing the fence and letting him know with another perfectly aimed barb just what the first one was supposed to mean. She didn't. She had all the advantages she needed right now. He was going to have to go to her and find out. "My leavin' didn't disappoint anybody around here too much," he reminded her as he scaled the fence. "People are glad to see me 'bout every two, three years, and for a week or so I'm glad to see them."

He swung one leg over the top rail and paused while she turned her face up to him. He wasn't sure he wanted to get down. Kenny was dead, and, damn, she scared him. He was afraid he would say something stupid, maybe make her cry. The cold autumn air had brought color to her face, but the dark shadows under her eyes canceled out the illusion of rosy-cheeked vitality. It struck him that her black down-filled jacket looked big enough to go around her twice. Then he realized it was Kenny's jacket. Brand-new the last time he'd seen him.

Her eyes held his fast as he lowered his foothold halfway down the fence, then dropped to the ground. His arms hung awkwardly at his sides. He imagined putting them around her, the way he wanted to, but her eyes offered no hint of permission. He flexed his fingers. They were stiff from the cold.

"Why did you buy those horses?" she asked quietly. "You didn't really want them."

"Why didn't you call me, Amy?" She glanced away. "Ed Shaeffer over at the bank always knows how to get hold of me in an emergency. He would have tracked me down if you'd just—"

"There was so much to do. There were so many details, so many—" She hugged herself, clutching the voluminous jacket around her. "There were many things I didn't handle as well as I should have. I was..." A faintly apologetic smile curved her mouth as she lifted her gaze to meet his again. "... quite unprepared."

"I stopped in at the house on my way into town." If he told her what he'd been through, maybe she would give him an answer that had something to do with *him*. "Stopped at the Jackalope. They talked about it like I already knew."

"I'm sorry." He looked away. "Really, Tate, I'm sorry. I thought about—" She laid her hand on his sleeve. "Many times I thought about writing, but I kept putting it off, thinking someone must have told you by now."

"I would have been back, soon as I heard. You would have seen me the same damn day." He stared at her hand. "That's why you kept puttin' it off, isn't it?"

"Oh, no. Ken would have wanted you to be..." He looked at her expectantly, waiting for the charge of a dead man. "To take part in the service."

"To help carry him to his grave? Damn right he would have. But I haven't been in touch since Christmas, and ol' Kenny, he usually—" The guilt was his. Always, it was his. "I should've known something was wrong."

"Tate." She slid her hand down his sleeve and slipped it in his. It felt good—warmer than his, and small but capable. "You come up with a list of regrets, and mine'll double yours. That's just the way it is. It was all over so quickly. So quickly, it left my head spinning."

A fleet, flighty gesture parted the front of her jacket. Her pink shirt was too tight. Her belly was too big. He felt as though he'd just walked up to her bedroom window and seen her naked.

"You're..." He was about to say something totally inane, and there wasn't a damn thing he could do about it. Gates were clattering inside the stock barn, and some guy was calling for lot forty-two. Tate glanced over his shoulder, unconsciously looking for somebody to tell him his eyes weren't lying. "Amy, you're pregnant."

"You're very observant."

"But they were saying over at—" He motioned westward, because suddenly he couldn't get the name of the bar out, or any other word that might offend her. The hand he held in his felt even slighter than it had at first, and he flexed his fingers around it, gently reasserting his hold. "I mean, I heard that you were running the place yourself."

"I'm not letting it go, Tate." And she squeezed back, a secret gesture between two people who shared a loss, letting him know that she was worried about losing still more. "It's my home. Mine and Jody's and..."

"You can't—"

"I'm having a baby, not open-heart surgery."

He allowed himself to get lost in the depths of her eyes, her brave words, her sturdiness. "You got any help?"

"I might be able to hire someone now, maybe part-time—" she smiled and gave a little nod toward the pen "—since I got a good price for those hay-burners."

"How's the little guy doin'? Jody?" She nodded to confirm the name he remembered full well. Kenny had once confided that Tate had been his choice for the boy's godfather, but with him on the rodeo circuit and Amy insisting on having the ceremony "before the little guy went to college," Tate had missed out on the honor.

Amy withdrew her hand, as though the mention of the boy's name had introduced a constraint against hand-holding. She stepped close to the pen and peeked between the rails again.

Tate followed her lead. "Must be tough for such a little fella," he said quietly. "Old enough to know the difference, but not to really..." *Understand?* Who *was* old enough to understand?

"He was pretty mad at me today. He used to love to come to the horse sales with his dad. This is the first one I've been to since...since it happened." She leaned her shoulder against the fence and hid her memories beneath lowered lashes. "I wouldn't let Jody come. He wouldn't understand."

Tate stared into the pen. The mare was standing hipshot, neck drooping, eyelids dropping to half-mast. The buckskin's perked ears rotated like radar as he blew thick clouds of mist through flaring nostrils. Whatever was up, the buckskin would be the first to know about it.

"The boy'll know they're gone," Tate said.

"Not right away." Amy sighed. "I didn't want him to watch them go through the ring."

"That must've been hard for you, too."

"Not at all. I'm glad to be rid of them." He glanced at her for an explanation. None was forthcoming. "What will you do with those two?" she wondered.

"Haven't given it much thought," he admitted. Then he smiled. "Just knew I couldn't pass 'em up."

"That's what Ken Becker would've said. Not Tate Harrison." He shrugged. She'd always thought she had them both pegged. "He missed you a lot, Tate," she added gently. "You were the brother he never had."

"He was—" He couldn't say that. He'd had a brother once, a long time ago. Jesse. But he'd grown up with Kenny. That, too, was beginning to seem like a long time ago. "He was the best friend I ever had.

Guess I should've missed him more than I did." He turned, leaned his back against the fence and looked up at the distant white clouds. "Guess I'm gonna start now."

"Well..." She wrapped her arms around herself again and they stood there for a long moment of silence, together but apart. One of the stockboys ran by, hollering at someone in the parking lot to wait up.

"How long will you be in town?" she finally asked. "You're welcome to come for supper, if you can find some time. You should see Jody now. He's..."

There it was, he thought. The obligatory invitation. "I'd wanna know more about what happened to Kenny," Tate warned her. "Would you be up to—" She hung her head. "That's okay. I understand. It's just that it's so hard for me to believe he's...gone."

"Dead. There's no way to change that, and that's all there is to know." She looked up, more fire in her eyes than he'd seen so far. "He's dead, Tate. It helps if you just say the word. It happened—" she snapped her fingers "—just like that. You can't believe how fast it happened, and you can't believe it happened until you've said the word. Until you've sold his horses. Until you've given most of his clothes away, and until you've slept..." She sighed, as if the sudden burst of emotion had worn her out. "I have to pick up Jody."

No, he didn't want her to go. He laid a hand on her shoulder. "What can I do?"

"Do?"

"For you and Jody. What—"

"You've already done more than you needed to do." She nodded toward the pen. "You've bought yourself one docile saddle horse and one mean outlaw. You'll have to figure out what you're going to do with *them*."

She kissed his cheek before she walked away. Made him feel like a little boy. Like she'd already come through the fires of hell, and he was too green to notice there was any heat. Even so, he felt favored somehow. Excused. Blessed. Knighted. Kissed by the princess. It was his cue to rise to the occasion.

He would do it if he knew how.

He decided he would run the mare back through the ring and keep the high-lifed buckskin gelding. The buckskin was obviously the outlaw, which made them two of a kind.

Jody was still mad when Amy picked him up at his aunt Marianne's. Cousin Kitty had slammed his finger in the car door, for one thing, and then Bill, Jr., had jerked the cherry sucker out of his mouth and made him bite his tongue. Marianne assured Amy that she'd checked him over both times and Jody wasn't really hurt. His tongue had hardly bled at all.

Then she'd asked Amy for the two hundredth time about the possibility of having core samples taken on her land, "Just to see if it's worth pursuing."

Amy wasn't interested in Ken's sister's latest scheme. The land Ken's father had left him belonged to her and Jody now. Marianne owned fifty percent of the mineral rights, which the attorney had explained was a technicality that would only become an issue if Amy decided either to sell the land or let people poke holes in it looking for something to mine. Neither proposition interested her, even though she knew one of Overo's poker clubs had a couple of betting pools going—one on her second child's birth date, and the other on the month in which she would file bankruptcy.

But Amy was not giving up. She was tired, and she was nearly broke, but she wouldn't be broken. Nobody was going to poke holes in Becker land or Becker dreams. Even if Ken's plans had frequently been far-fetched, he'd been fond of saying that he could depend on Amy to get him turned around. Once he was headed in the right direction, he could make things happen. He could be hell on wheels, he would say. He'd spent much of their marriage spinning his wheels, but she'd known how and when to wedge her small shoulder under his axle and give him a push. He was a good man, a kind-hearted man and he had wonderful intentions. Amy's job was to find a kernel of feasibility in them and build on that.

So at least they had a ranch. It might not have been the kind of ranch Ken had envisioned, but they were raising livestock. They had a home. They had a family. Despite a few impulsive choices, a few setbacks, a few fits and starts, they had come *this* far. Now it was up to her. It hadn't been easy without Ken, but there had been times when it hadn't been easy *with* him, either. Amy would manage, just as she had always managed. She would just have to work harder.

But she did need a little help. Now that she had some money, she needed manpower. A couple of months' worth, she figured. She could have given birth to a new baby, looked after a four-year-old and tended to her business in the summer, no sweat. But winter in Montana could throw a fast-frozen kink into anybody's works.

She wouldn't let herself think about where the money had come from until after she had put Jody to bed and her feet up on two feather pillows and a hassock. It wouldn't have been so hard to sell Ken's saddle horse—especially that outlaw that had been the death of him—if the buyer hadn't turned out to be Tate Harrison. But there was probably some kind of poetic justice in it all. She'd never doubted that she would have to face Tate sooner or later.

In that first rush of confusion, the initial daze and the onslaught of questions and decisions, her first impulse had been to find Tate. It had been a foolish idea, and she'd rebuked whatever infirm hormone it was that had bombarded her brain with such a weak-kneed notion. She'd breathed the biggest sigh of relief of her life the day Tate Harrison had left Overo and all but removed his freewheeling influence from her husband's life. She didn't really know how to get hold of him, not easily, not on such short notice, and he probably wouldn't have been free to come. He would come home for a party, but for a funeral? She doubted it. Or rather, she elected to doubt it. It was simpler that way.

But, as fate would have it, she'd had to face him with her excuses right after he'd done his good deed. As if that weren't bad enough, she'd had to deal with those *stupid* feelings again. Tate Harrison always made her feel a little unsteady, slightly unsafe, as though she'd pitched camp on a geological fault. He made her want to do things she shouldn't do, just the way he had Ken. There was a look in his eyes, a challenge to be as bold and as rash as he was.

Even in sorrow, he challenged her. It would have been easy to let herself go, to break down in his arms. That was probably exactly what he expected—what everyone expected. It was also exactly the kind of behavior in which Amy could ill afford to indulge herself. She had responsibilities.

It was late when she heard the pickup drive up. She turned in her chair just as the headlights played over the sheers in the front window. Someone was probably stopping to tell her that that damned west gate was open again. She sighed and hauled herself to her feet. The dogs were going nuts outside. She would show them; she'd put them to work. Thank God she had the dogs.

Amy turned the porch light on, then peeked out the window. The face that peered back was disturbingly familiar. The angles softened earlier by daylight looked harder in the shadows, the bristly stubble darker, the black eyes less forgiving and the full, firm lips less patient. It was not the kind of face one welcomed late at night. But she unlocked the door.

Tate felt like the third guy from the left in a police lineup as he stood there waiting. Frost was nipping at his nose while she was looking him over, being none too quick about opening the damn door.

"Oh, Tate." She made his name sound like a protest against any and all surprises. "Come in. We've already eaten, and Jody's—" She shrank back, as though he were muscling his way into her cozy nest.

Feeling awkward and a bit oversize for the small entryway, he stepped over the threshold, tucking his chin as he removed his hat.

"But I can heat something up for you," she added tentatively.

"I didn't come for supper, exactly." He fingered his Stetson's broad black brim. "I'm lookin' for a job."

"A job?" She laughed nervously. Standing there in her dimly-lit kitchen, he looked for all the world like a hulking, humble cowboy. "Did you blow all your money on those horses?" She knew all about that little routine from Kenny. Tate had his foolish habits, but burdening himself with useless horses was not one of them.

"I've got money," he assured her. "What I need is a place to stay for a while."

"Try the motel." She didn't mean to sound sarcastic, but the wounded expression on his face told her that it had come out that way.

"I've had a bellyful of motels." He squared his shoulders and nodded toward the door that led to the basement. "You've got a room downstairs. You need a hired man."

"I don't need—" she took a deep breath while his eyes dared her to effect a complete rejection "—a favor quite that big."

"It won't be a favor. I'm not an easy keeper. I eat a lot and I, uh—" he glanced past her, surveying the homey kitchen "—use a lot of hot water."

"I can't pay you much more than that."

"All I'm askin' for is room and board." He shoved his hands in the front pockets of his jeans and offered a lopsided grin. "And all the shells to the shotgun."

"You heard about that." With few exceptions, she'd always been good at setting people straight. Tate Harrison was one of the few she'd had trouble with. "That happened back in June. I'm a little slower now, but you still won't get any further than he did, so don't—"

"You've got a belly sittin' out there as big as a four-way stop sign." The amusement in his eyes faded. "That's all you need, Amy. A big red stop sign."

Ah, so he remembered. Well, so did she. She'd never told Ken about the time Tate had made his move on her, partly because it had happened before they were married and mostly because she had handled it. There had never been a need to discuss the incident. It would have served no purpose other than to prove that she had been right about Tate. He, of course, had been wrong about her, and he'd admitted it. So maybe it wouldn't hurt to let him help out for a while. Nobody had ever suggested that Tate Harrison wasn't a hard worker when he wanted to be.

And from the spark that flashed in his eyes when she relented with a reluctant nod, he wanted to be.

"You're right. I need a hand," she said. "One I can trust. As long as you have some free time..."

He read the question in her eyes. "I can spare as much as you need."

"I promise you, Tate, I bounce back fast. I did with Jody."

"Every time I laid over with you guys, even for a day or two, I felt like you were in a rush to kick me out." It was an observation, not a complaint. "I'd try to get you both out of the house, take you out to supper or just honky-tonkin', and you always acted like I was—"

"Ken had responsibilities," she reminded him, although it wasn't something she expected a confirmed bachelor like Tate to understand. She smiled. "If it's any comfort, it was nothing personal. You weren't the only rowdy sidekick I ever bitched out royally."

"Admit it." He gave her a sly wink. "I always got your best shot."

"You earned it."

"I'll get my gear." He stepped back and put his hat back on. "First thing tomorrow morning, it'll give me a world of pleasure to run those flea-bitten bleaters off your land."

"You mean the sheep?"

"Must be a hole in the fence somewhere," he judged. "Either that or—"

"Oh, Tate." There it was again. *Oh, Tate.* This time the coolness was missing. In fact, he'd apparently said something delightfully funny, which was fine with him. He liked the rich sound of her laughter and the way her belly bounced with it.

She touched her hand to her lips, then to his leather sleeve. "Those are *our* sheep, cowboy. You just hired on as a sheepherder."

Chapter Two

Long before Amy had become Ken's wife, Tate Harrison had been his best friend. She remembered the earlier days well, but not, she had to admit, without a certain small niggling of dissatisfaction with herself, a sense that she had been tested and found wanting. It was not the only time in her life that her behavior had come up short, of course, and it would surely not be the last. She was only human.

More irritating, though, was that little voice inside her head that always had the last say when she thought about those old bygones. Same voice, same taunting tone, always suggesting that she had also been *left* wanting. But the idea was perfectly foolish, absolutely irrational. Amy Becker was nothing if not prudent. She always had been, even back then....

* * *

From Glendive to Missoula, Tate's reputation as a heartbreaking hell-raiser had been legend. Amy had never been interested in men like Tate. She much preferred his friend Ken Becker, whom she'd met when she'd worked at a bank in Billings. When she'd become the head bookkeeper at the small branch in Overo, Ken had come courting. He'd seemed to think his role as bronc rider Tate Harrison's shadow was his best calling card. "We're gonna watch ol' Tate buck one out, and then we'll party," he would say.

It was hard to convince Ken that the best date he could plan with her was a picnic atop one of the beautiful red clay bluffs on his ranch east of the Absaroka foothills. He hadn't been running the place very long, and his goals for his ranching business seemed a bit scattered. But he'd been born to the business, she thought almost enviously. He was the third generation of Becker cattlemen on Becker land. He had the kind of roots Amy craved, and he needed her. She liked that. He was as impressed with her good sense as he was with her good figure. She liked that, too.

Tate Harrison, on the other hand, never seemed to meet a woman who didn't impress him somehow. But it never lasted long. Too often, Amy's dates with Ken would start out as a threesome, and then Tate would pick up a fourth somewhere along the way. Usually it was some empty-headed buckle bunny who couldn't smile prettily and carry on a conversation at the same time, so she would quickly give up on the latter.

The worst of that ilk was Patsy Johnson. Unfortunately, she lasted the longest. She loved to play with the buttons on his shirt and sip on his beer. She never wanted a cigarette of her own, but she was always taking a puff off Tate's. Whenever she did it, she always glanced at Amy, as if to say, *What's his is mine.* As if Amy cared. Amy wasn't interested in Tate's buttons. She didn't like beer. She didn't smoke. Ken had virtually quit, too, except when he was around Tate. In fact, the whole two-stepping, partner-swinging honky-tonk scene seemed to revolve around Tate, and Amy's little bottom simply wasn't comfortable on a bar stool.

One night she decided she'd had it with the rowdy cowboy-bar scene, where the soft drinks were too expensive, the music too loud and the women too cute. Ken and his friends were absolutely right; she did not know how to have a good time, and she didn't want to interfere with theirs. She made a trip to the ladies' room, then put in a phone call to solve her transportation problem. Enough of this noise, she told herself as she hung up the phone.

"Did you just call for a ride?"

Tate's voice startled her. Her heartbeat skipped into overdrive, and she had to remind herself that he wasn't catching her doing anything underhanded, which was almost the way she felt.

"Yes, I did," she said calmly as she turned to find him standing too close for comfort in the narrow hallway. The bare overhead light bulb cast his face in sharp light and deep shadows, playing up its chiseled angles. The knowing look in his eyes was unsettling. She was glad she had genuine justification, even if she didn't owe him any. "I have a headache."

"Does Kenny know?"

"He seems to be having an especially good time." Ken knew how to enjoy himself, which was part of what made him so likable, and when he was drinking, he enjoyed himself beyond Amy's ability to keep up. "And we came with you tonight, so I called—"

"Did he do something?" Amy shook her head quickly, and Tate laid his hand on his own chest. "Did *I* do something? I said something wrong," he supposed in all sincerity. "If it was that little joke about women in tight pants, I'm sorry. It didn't apply to you. I've never seen you wear—"

"It has nothing to do with anything you said. I just can't..." It seemed strange, but she felt as though she could level with him, now that it was just the two of them. He was looking at her intently, as though he were concerned about the fact that she felt so out of place sitting at a table with ashtrays overflowing with cigarette butts and an accumulation of empty beer bottles. "I'm not very good at this kind of thing." She gave a helpless gesture, the kind she generally scorned. "The loud music, the smoke ... sometimes it gives me a headache, that's all."

"All you have to do is say something, and we'll—"

"No, just let me—" She touched her fingertips to her throbbing temple. "I don't want to break up the party. I just want to go home."

"Come on." He put one hand on her shoulder, guiding her toward the side door as he shoved his other hand in his pocket. She shook her head, trying to demur, but he cut her off. "No, I'll take you. It's no trouble."

"But I've already called—"

"I'll take care of it. Kenny's sister, right?" She nodded.

Reassuring her with a light squeeze of his hand, he signaled the woman who'd been waiting on their table. "Jeri, honey, call Marianne and tell her Amy found another ride. And tell Kenny I'll be back in half an hour, that Amy's okay, but she needs to get home right away." He glanced at their empty table as he tucked some money into Jeri's hand. Kenny and Patsy had taken to the dance floor.

Tate put Amy in his pickup and headed across town to the small house she'd rented. It was tiny, but it was the first real house she'd ever lived in. She'd had her own apartment in Billings, and before that she'd lived in apartments and trailer homes with her family. She'd always wanted a real house.

"It's a relief to breathe fresh air," she told Tate. It was also a surprise to her to hear herself confiding, "I feel like a fifth wheel sometimes, especially when Ken has too much to drink." Too quickly she added, "Which he doesn't, usually."

"Well, I'm driving tonight, so Ken doesn't have to worry about having himself a good time."

She didn't understand their definition of having a good time, especially when it was bound to turn into a hangover by morning. "He's beyond the point where it would do any good to ask him to call it a night."

"Did you try?"

"'Just one more,' he said."

"Kenny's crazy about you, you know." He seemed to think he'd offered some great revelation, and he paused to let it sink in before he added, "He's making a lot of big plans. Not that it's any of my business."

"It is your business." Her tone betrayed her resentment. "Whatever his plans are, you'll know all about them before I do."

"We go back a long way, Kenny and me. A guy's gotta talk things out with a close buddy sometimes, especially when he's not too sure what's gonna happen." He dropped his hand and downshifted for a right turn. "He's afraid you'll turn him down." He kept his eyes on the road ahead, shifted again and surprised her by adding, "I'm afraid you won't."

"You think I'd spoil all the fun?" she asked scornfully, but Tate said nothing as he pulled over in front of her house. "There's more to life than rodeos and smoke-filled bars. If that's all you want, then fine, but I think Ken needs—"

"You're probably just what Kenny needs." Tate shut off the ignition, draped his left arm over the steering wheel and turned to her. "But he's not the kind of man you need. Deep down, I think you know that."

"He's a wonderful man," Amy insisted, reflexively bristling in Ken's defense. "He has a good sense of humor and the kindest heart and the gentlest nature of any man I've ever—" she paused and lifted her chin, defying the smile that tugged at the corner of Tate's mouth, for her concluding word came all too quietly "—met."

"You're right about that. Kenny's a nice guy." He laid his right arm along the top of the seat and touched her shoulder lightly. "You'll walk all over him. And he'll let you do it, because when you're done, he'll just pick himself up and do as he pleases. He'll do all that nice-guy stuff he likes to do, the stuff that never amounts to anything and never gets him anywhere. And you'll cover for him, which means he'll be walkin' all over you in his nice-guy way." In the dim light his eyes were completely overshadowed by the brim of his black cowboy hat, but she could feel them studying her. "Is that what you want?" he asked.

She answered tightly. "That's not the way it would be."

"Like I said, Kenny and me . . ." He shoved his hat back with his thumb and stretched lazily. "We go back a long, long way."

"You said you thought he was crazy about me."

"I *know* he's crazy about you. I know what Kenny thinks long before *he* does." He chuckled. "It won't take you very long to achieve that skill. You're probably halfway there already."

"With friends like you, he certainly doesn't need any enemies."

"I am his friend. I'd back him in the devil's own ambush, and he'd do the same for me." He glanced past the windshield at a pair of oncoming headlights. The car cruised by, and Tate shook his head, smiling wistfully. "But if I was a woman, I sure as hell wouldn't wanna be married to him."

"You wouldn't want to be married to anyone. That's why you go out with women like Patsy Johnson, who'll sit there and rub your thigh while she giggles at every word you say, whether it's supposed to be funny or not. She doesn't expect you to marry her."

"What does she expect?"

"You know what she expects," Amy snapped.

Tate chuckled. "Which part bothers you most? I don't like to be laughed at when I'm not joking, and when I am, you usually laugh, too. So you've got no reason to be jealous there."

"Jealous!"

"But it's hard to resist a woman who's got her hand on your thigh." His amused tone rankled almost as much as his male complacency. "'Specially if you've got no good reason to." He slid closer. "If you wanted to, you could give me a good reason to resist Patsy or any other woman."

"Why would I want to do that?" She knew what a dumb question it was. Dumber still was her willingness to sit still for the answer.

"Because you wanna be the one rubbin' my thigh."

He was smiling, looking just about as irresistible as any man who'd ever donned a Stetson, and she was melting like ice cream in July. She imagined slapping her own cheek to wake herself up, but it was more fascinating to watch him take off his hat and balance it between the dashboard and the steering wheel.

"You know this for a fact?" she asked, fully realizing that this banter was part of the game and she was just taking her silly turn.

"Sure do." He took her shoulders in his hands and turned her to him. "And you want me to be the one takin' you home, because you know damn well you'd never have to ask me twice."

He slowly pulled her close, challenging her to deny the truth in his claim, refusing to let her gaze stray from his. He'd brought her home, hadn't he? The house was only a few yards away, and she was still sitting there. She wanted his kiss, didn't she? When he brushed his palm against the side of her face and slid his fingers into her hair, she knew he was giving her all the time she needed to say otherwise. She couldn't. She parted her lips, but no words would come.

He hooked one arm around her shoulders, lowered his head and kissed her, softly at first, then more insistently, pressing for her response. Her mouth yielded to his as her breath fluttered wildly in her chest. His tongue touched hers like a sportsman testing the direction of the wind. Ah, yes, he seemed to say, that's the way of it, and he turned his head to try another angle.

She liked the sweet whiskey taste of him and the woody scent of his after-shave. His slim waist seemed a good place to put her hand. Her touch was his signal to draw her closer and kiss her harder. He rubbed her back with the heels of his hands, relaxing her, melting her spine, vertebra by vertebra. Then he slipped his hand between their bodies, cupping one breast in his palm while he insinuated his fingertips past her V-neck blouse and stroked the soft swell of its twin. Both nipples tightened in response.

She leaned into his embrace and answered his tongue's probing with the flickerings of hers. She wanted to be closer still. She wanted to feel his hand inside her blouse, skin against warm skin. She wanted to let him guide her, let him show her the way to lose herself in her own senses. Slowly she slid her hand up his long, hard back, up to his shoulder, where she gripped him as though she were teetering and needed support. He groaned, and his kiss became more urgent, more hungry.

"Let's go inside," he whispered.

"Oh, Tate." She wanted to. But making a move required her to open her eyes and realize that she was in the arms of a man who was more than attractive, far beyond adequate and a notch past willing. He was ready to meet her demands, but he would have his own ideas, as well. And he was not Ken.

Ken. The man she was supposed to be with tonight.

"Oh my God. No, Tate, this is all wrong." And it suddenly scared the hell out of her.

Her reluctance didn't seem to surprise him. "It'll be all right once you get it straight in your mind what you really want," he said evenly.

"I want a home. I want a family." Pulling back from him wasn't easy, so she resorted to the kind of ammunition she knew would scare a man like Tate off. "I want love first and then . . . and *then* sex. Ken—"

It was the name that did it. Tate's shoulders sagged a little as his embrace slackened. Amy closed her eyes and fought the urge to close her hands around his retreating arms before they got away completely. She had to say it again quickly. She had to *hear* it again. "*Ken* and I don't . . ."

"That's not something we talk over, whether you do or you don't. I'm not interested in hearing any of that," he snapped as he closed his hand around her left wrist and lifted her hand in front of her own face.

"You're not wearing his ring. That's all I need to know."

Six months later Tate had known all he'd needed to. He'd carried the small gold band to the altar in his breast pocket, then turned it over to his best friend. He'd witnessed their vows, stood by while they were sealed with a kiss, even put his signature on the official documents. Amy wondered if his participation was Tate's way of backing Ken in "the devil's own ambush." He had kissed the bride properly in his turn and waltzed her once around the Overo Community Hall dance floor. It was the one time Amy could remember that Tate had left the party early—and alone.

On the first morning after he'd talked himself into the lowest-paying job he'd ever had, Tate was lured up the basement stairs by the commingling aromas of bacon and coffee. It had been a long time since he'd been up before the roosters, but he wanted to get started on the right foot with his new boss. He took it as a good sign when she glanced up from the big iron skillet and greeted him with a bright smile, never missing a beat as she turned a row of flapjacks, golden brown side up. It pleased him that she remembered his breakfast preferences.

"Sheep, huh?" He smiled back as he poured himself a cup of strong black coffee.

"Sheep."

"How many head?"

"Three hundred. And they pay the bills." The metal spatula scraped lightly against the skillet as she started dishing out the pancakes. "I can handle sheep, whereas I wasn't much help with the cattle."

"And cattle were the best excuse Kenny could think of for keeping horses around." Tate took a seat at the kitchen table.

"He really just wanted to raise horses, which would have been fine if—"

"If they'd paid the bills."

"Exactly." She wasn't fussy. She intended to keep her home intact. She would raise earthworms if the price were right. "Ken and I made a deal two years ago when he was beginning to realize that my little herd of sheep was more profitable than his whole—"

"You're a better businessperson than Kenny was," Tate said, cutting to the crux of the matter. "Did he ever realize *that* somewhere along the line?"

"Yes, he did. We all have our talents. Anyway, I agreed to the horses, and he agreed to the sheep. We got out of the cattle business."

"Sheep." The traditional bane of the cattleman. Not that Tate was in a position to care all that much, since he didn't own any cattle anymore, just a parcel of land, and it didn't appear that she'd used it to graze sheep. The damn woollies could crop the grass down halfway to China if a stockman didn't use a good rotation plan.

But here he was, offering his personal services, which would mean personal contact. He preferred the smell of cattle over the stink of sheep any day. He thought about it as he sipped his coffee. Finally he shook his head. "Well, you can give my portion of mutton to the dogs and double my ration of hot water."

"I don't serve mutton."

She *did* serve a nice plate of flapjacks and bacon, though, and he took a deep whiff as she set it down in front of him.

"Thank God for small favors. I'm going to have to fix that shower stall before I use it." He tasted the crisp bacon, then elaborated. "It doesn't drain right."

"I usually just mop up the water." The resignation in her voice irritated him. She planted her knuckles against her hip as she turned back to the stove. Her little fist was dwarfed by the basketball of a belly that tested the limits of her pretty pink sweater. "Ken was going to fix that shower, but there were other repairs that were higher on the priority list."

Tate imagined her down on her hands and knees, wiping the floor with a towel. "You give me the list," he ordered as he cut into the stack of flapjacks with his fork. "And a mop, if you don't want me to use your shower upstairs this morning." She wasn't mopping up *his* water.

"You're welcome to use the upstairs bathroom. Just let me check to make sure I've got clean soap and dry—"

"Clean soap?"

"You know, *fresh*. And towels, and Jody's bath toys out of the way."

"Does he have boats? Maybe I'll take a bath instead." He was chuckling happily. She wasn't. He could see her adding another chore to her mental list. "Amy, soap is soap, and I can find the towels. I don't need any special treatment, okay? I'm the hired hand, not a guest from out of town."

"Housekeeping hasn't been tops on my list of priorities lately, but ordinarily—"

"I don't see anything out of place," he assured her. And then, as if on cue, a sleepy-eyed blond moppet appeared in the kitchen doorway. "Hey, who's this big guy?" Tate laughed when his dubious greeting sent the boy scurrying to his mother's side. "Are you the same Jody who used to twist my ear half off when I gave him horseyback rides?"

The little boy looked up at his mother for some hint as to how he was supposed to answer.

"Do you remember Tate, sweetheart? Daddy's good friend?"

Tate, sweetheart. He smiled, enjoying the way it sounded. "You were a little squirt last time I was here, but you sure are getting big."

"I'm almost five," Jody announced bravely as he flashed splayed fingers Tate's way. "If I coulda' been five in August, I'd be in kindergarten."

"Well, next year. You must be big enough to ride a two-wheeler. I almost tripped over one out by the yard fence. Is that yours?"

"It *was* Bill, Jr.'s." Jody ventured a few cautious steps from his mother's side. "I'm gonna give it back to him," he added, clearly for Amy's edification.

"You'll get the hang of it, Jody. Maybe we'll put it away until spring." Amy sighed. "By then it won't be quite so hard for me to get you going."

"You just learning?" Tate asked as Jody joined him at the table.

"I keep falling off when my mom lets go. I'd rather ride a horse."

"I'm with you there, partner. If your mom'll let me use the horse trailer, I'll head into town after I get some chores done around here and bring back your dad's—"

"Breakfast first." Amy cast Tate a warning glance as she plunked a glass of orange juice on the table for Jody.

"My dad's what?"

"Your dad's . . ."

"Tate is going to help us out for a while, Jody, and he needed a horse, so I sold him—"

"The buckskin," Tate supplied. "That's the one I—" wrong choice, obviously, the way she was rolling her eyes "—kept. He moves out spirited and stylish, and he's got a nice head on him, good chest. The mare was kinda goose-rumped and paunchy." He eyed Amy playfully. "Like mares get sometimes."

"Very funny." Both hands went to her hips as Jody slipped away from the table. "In other words, you weren't about to listen to me."

"I know good horseflesh," Tate pointed out quietly. He hoped Jody wasn't beating feet down the hallway because of something he'd said. He'd just wanted the boy to know that his dad's horse would still be around.

"The buckskin was Ken's favorite, too," Amy said.

"So you were down to the four?"

"No. There are eighteen registered quarter horses out there. The mares aren't bred. The geldings aren't broke. You might say we're horse-poor. I can't afford to keep them, can't afford to give them away." She shook her head sadly. "Not Ken's dream herd."

"Horse-poor, huh," Tate echoed reflectively.

Jody reappeared, carrying a broken stick horse with a missing ear.

"Whatcha got there, partner?" Tate asked. Jody handed over his steed. "Does this guy have a little better handle than that two-wheeler? Looks like he got hogged." Tate ran his hand over the remains of a yarn mane, which had obviously been cut short by an inexperienced groom.

"I buzzed him with the scissors. He's glass-eyed, see?" Jody pointed to the pony's eye, which was indeed made of glass, but a horseman would term him glass-eyed because it was blue. "But whoever heard of a horse with blue-and-white polka dots?"

"You've never seen a blue roan?"

"That's not a roan."

"Looks like a roan to me." Tate turned the stick in his hand as he examined what was clearly a well-loved toy. "I think I can fix him up for you. Do a little fancy blacksmithin'." He winked at the boy, who listened spellbound at his knee. "And we can probably get that bike of yours at least green-broke while I'm here. When you get throwed, best thing is to climb back into the saddle."

"Ready for pancakes, Jody?"

"Soon as I put Thunder back in his stall."

After the little boy had galloped out of earshot, Amy turned from the stove, plate in hand. "Don't make him any more promises, Tate. Two is enough. He's pretty confused as it is."

"I don't make empty promises." His look challenged her to disagree. When she didn't, he glanced away. "He looks a lot like his dad."

"Yes, he does. And now he reminds me of Peter Pan's shadow, sort of at loose ends." In another part of the house a closet door was opened, then shut. Amy set Jody's plate on the table and spoke softly. "Just be careful. I'm afraid he's looking for a man's boots to attach his little feet to."

"You think I'm gonna drag that little guy along behind me?" He reached for his coffee. "That's not my way, Amy."

"What is your way?"

"With kids?" Tate shrugged. "I don't know. I'm a little short on experience. Just be a friend and stick around while times are tough, I guess. Is that okay?" She nodded, and he smiled. "Good. So far his size doesn't scare me much. Long as I don't have to get on that two-wheeler myself, I'll be all right."

The autumn grass provided the sheep with plenty of roughage, but they needed supplemental feed. Amy laid out her instructions to the letter before turning the chore over to "the guys." Tate shoveled a load of grain into the pickup bed and took Jody along to show him where the feeders were. The sheep trotted across the pasture, bleating to beat hell when they saw the pickup coming.

Tate pulled up to one of the scattered feeders and set about filling the trough with grain. For an almost-five-year-old, Jody seemed pretty grown-up. He often mirrored what Tate recognized as Amy's instructive manner. "We have to spread it out in the trough so they won't climb all over each other," the boy said soberly as he put his small hands to the task.

"Who's been hauling this out to the sheep since the last man quit?" They'd probably been supplementing for a month or more, Tate figured. He stood back and watched the dingy white merino ewes jostle for position around the trough.

"Me and Mom." Jody squinted one eye against the glare of the morning sun. "We're not as strong as you, so it takes a long time. We put the feed in a lot of small things, like ice-cream buckets, load them up in the pickup and—" with a gesture he drew a beeline in the sky "—buzz on out here. Did you know we're gonna have a baby? That's why my mom has such a big tummy."

"You mean it's not always that big?"

"No, that's a baby inside her. A little baby about—" he held his little round hands inches apart "—I'd say this big. That's why Mom had to stop using the scoop shovel to load the grain. Her big tummy got in the way."

Tate forced a chuckle for Jody's benefit, but it pinched his throat. He thought about Amy wielding that big shovel, and he shook his head. "Brother or sister, do you know?"

"No, that's going to be a surprise. I'm hoping for a brother."

"But a sister would be nice, too. Right?"

"I don't know." Jody scowled, then thrust his hand up for Tate's inspection. "My cousin Kitty slammed the car door on my finger yesterday. See?"

Tate hunkered down behind the open tailgate and studied the purpling fingernail. "Does it still hurt? It looks like it must've hurt like a bit—" *Wrong choice of words.* "*Biddy.* Like an old biddy with a baseball bat, right? Boy, that can be murder."

"What's a biddy? Is it a girl, like my dumb ol' cousin Kitty?"

"Yeah. Only older and meaner." He smiled. This curly-haired little fellow was cuter than a spotted colt. "You might get a new fingernail out of this deal. Did your mom tell you that?"

"No." Incredulous, Jody took a closer look at his finger. "You mean my fingernail might fall off?"

"After a while. But it'll be okay, because you'll get a new one. It's happened to me a lot of times."

"By a biddy hittin' you with a bat?"

"By getting my hand caught in a door or stomped by a horse or banged with a hammer." He ruffled the boy's cotton-candy curls as he stood. "It's not always a girl's fault."

"I still want a brother," Jody insisted.

"Either way, you'll have a new baby." Tate tossed the shovel into the pickup bed.

"Do you know about babies?" Jody wondered.

"I know they don't play much for the first year or so, and then they start gettin' into things. Have you had pups around, or kittens?" Jody nodded vigorously. "Kinda like that. Brothers get to be more fun when they get a little age on 'em."

"But he plays around in my mom's tummy right now," Jody disclosed as he followed Tate to the driver's side.

Tate pictured an unborn child "playing around" in a warm, dark, cozy haven. He smiled as he hoisted Jody into the pickup. "What does he play?"

"He kicks." Jody scrambled over on the bench seat to make room for the driver. "Sometimes Mom says it feels like he's playing football. She lets me feel it, too. He kicked my nose once when I was just tryin' to talk to him in there."

Tate was still smiling as he buckled Jody's seat belt.

"Next time I'll let you feel, too," Jody offered magnanimously.

"Feel what?"

"The baby kicking."

"Oh, well, your mom might, uh…" Let him put his hand on her belly? Yeah, right. But he was *still* smiling. "She might have something to say about that."

"She'll let you. She always lets me."

When they got back to the barn, they found Amy raking out stalls. Her long, chestnut-colored hair was clipped back at the nape, but bits of it had strayed over her face as she worked. She'd tossed Kenny's black parka aside and pushed up the sleeves of her pink sweater. She looked up when she heard them coming, then leaned on the rake handle as she pressed her free hand against the small of her back.

"Whew, I'm working up a sweat here." She wiped her brow with the back of her hand. "Lately it doesn't take much and I'm all in a sweat."

"Go back in the house, Amy. I know where everything is, and I swear to you I've already got the hang of the routine down pat. Jody and me—" She wasn't listening. She'd slid her hand over her ripe, round belly and gotten a funny look on her face. "What's the matter?"

"Is he kickin' again, Mom?"

"*She*—" Amy put her hand under Jody's up-turned chin and offered a motherly smile "—is going to be a Rockette. The little rascal is in top form to-day."

"Where, where, where?" Jody jumped up and down like a pogo-stick rider until Amy took hold of his hand and placed it against the lower left side of her stomach. "Yow! Mom, that baby kicked me again," Jody chirped. "Let Tate feel."

Bubbling with excitement, Jody was puzzled by the sudden stillness. He looked up at one face, then the other, and he wondered at his power. He'd just cre-ated two awkwardly flash-frozen big people, staring dumbly at each other. "Come on, Tate wants to feel, dontcha, Tate?"

"Jody, my hands are pretty—" Tate looked down at hands that might have belonged to someone else, as awkward as they suddenly felt. He flexed his fingers as though he were working out some stiffness in the joints. "They're too dirty and...too cold."

"He won't know that," the boy assured him with exaggerated patience. "He's inside Mom's tummy." He claimed Tate's big, rugged, reluctant hand in his small but sure one. "Where do you feel it now, Mom?"

"Here," Amy said softly. She leaned back against a short stack of square bales as she reached for Tate's hand.

Her skin felt like a firebrick against his. He tipped his hat back with one finger as he sought and found her permission in her soulful, brown, earth-mother eyes. He swallowed convulsively. She directed his hand, pressing it against her as though she were showing him where to find her most personal, most intimate secret. Her belly was harder than he had thought it would be, and wondrously round, like a perfect piece of fruit. He wanted to slip his hand under the sweater—damn pesky wool—and touch taut, smooth skin, but not in an invasive way. More like reverent. It was sure corny, but that was the way he felt. He'd almost forgotten what he was supposed to be feeling *for* until the little critter he couldn't see actually *moved* beneath his hand.

"Ho-ly..." Without thinking, he went down on one knee. As though he were gazing into a crystal ball, he focused his whole attention on this precious part of Amy, the part that held her baby, the part that she permitted *him* to hold in his two hands.

"Hey, Mom, there's Cinnamon Toast." Jody pointed at the feline face peering down at them from the rafters. Neither Amy nor Tate flickered an eyelash. "C'mere, Cinnamon," Jody coaxed as he headed up the ladder to the loft.

"Is that a foot?" Tate asked quietly, afraid he might scare whatever was in there, whatever, *whoever*, seemed to be responding to his touch.

"What does it feel like to you?"

"Like somebody tryin' to fight his way out of a—" He looked into her eyes and gave a teasing half smile. "A balloon?"

"Tactful choice."

"Does he do this all the time?"

"I think she's one of those children who loves to perform for an audience."

"Jeez, she's really—" he moved his hand, following the movement within Amy "—goin' to town here. How long before she's supposed to make her appearance?"

"Three weeks. But you can give or take two. Jody was late. But, then, I know when this one got her start, almost to the hour."

They shared a solemn look. Then an oppressive thought hit Tate like a cannonball. She was speaking of an hour he didn't want to think too much about, not just because it had been one of Kenny's last, but because . . . because he'd made himself stop thinking about the two of them in that way a long time ago, and he didn't want to start in again. He drew his hands away gradually as he rose from the straw-covered floor.

"Ken never knew," Amy said.

"He knows now."

"Do you believe that?"

"Sure." He sought to put some distance between himself and the bone-melting experience he'd just had by remembering his friend the way he ought to have been remembering him. "I can't see him wearin' a halo or any of that kind of stuff, but I believe he's in a good place, and I think he'll be with you in spirit." Her eyes took on a misty sheen, and her brave smile consecrated his amended efforts. Damn, he could talk nice when he saw a need. "Especially when the baby's born," he added. "I think he'll be there, come hell or high water." He laid a comforting hand on her shoulder. "So to speak."

"So to speak," she echoed softly.

He nodded, and his eyes strayed to her distended belly again. "That's pretty amazing. I mean, you don't realize how amazing until you actually..." He extended his hand impulsively, then arrested the presumptuous move to touch her stomach once more, turning it into an empty-handed gesture. "That's pretty amazing."

"You're blushing, Tate Harrison." He glanced at her, then glanced away, shaking his head. "Yes, you are. You are as pink as—"

Tate chuckled, genuinely embarrassed. *Damn.* Where had this big, dumb cowboy come from? Hadn't he just been doing the silver-tongued knight like a seasoned pro?

"You look like a newborn with a five o'clock shadow." She cupped his bristly cheek in her small hand. "*That* is pretty amazing."

Chapter Three

Tate's plan was to get in a few chores before breakfast, but Amy had already foiled it three days running. The woman didn't know how to sleep in. He
could have sworn it was still the middle of the night,
but she had him waking up to the smell of coffee. Her
time was getting close. Surely she needed more rest.
Each time he heard those early-morning footsteps
overhead, his first thought was, *Maybe this is it.*

Nah, couldn't be. If anything serious had started,
she wouldn't be fooling with the coffeepot at whatever the hell time it was. In order to see the time, he
would have to turn the damn light on. He would find
out soon enough. He dragged himself out of bed and
felt his way to the bathroom door. Once he'd stood in
the shower long enough to steam his eyes open, the

smell of her coffee drew him up the steps to the kitchen table.

"Oh, did I wake you up?" Amy asked sweetly. "I'm sorry. I really was trying to be quiet."

"You wanna be sneakin' around, you need a different pair of shoes," he told her, his mood lightening gradually. Her hair hung over her shoulder in one thick braid. He liked her light floral, fresh-from-the-shower scent. He also liked the way their fingers touched when she handed him his coffee.

"Ken gave me these." She lifted her foot and glanced down at the plastic heel on her slipper. "They're noisy?"

"Like Mr. Bojangles found a linoleum cloud in heaven."

"I'm hardly that light on my feet," she said with a laugh as she set a plate in front of him. "But see if these scrambled eggs are light and fluffy enough for you. How are you getting along with the dogs?"

"We're on speaking terms." The eggs went down easy. With a wink and a nod, he told her so. "I tell 'em, 'Speak,' and they say, 'Grrr-ruff.' Kinda mean-like, so my guess is we're speaking about territory, and they're tellin' me this is theirs."

"Don't take it personally. They didn't like Ken, either. Do you think you could bring the herd in by yourself?"

"You're talkin' to a professional cowboy here, ma'am." He smiled as she joined him at the table. "Among other things. If I can work cows, I sure as hell don't need any help bringin' in the sheep."

"Good. You'll bring them in, the dogs and I will sort them and we'll take the rest of the lambs to the sale barn tomorrow."

"I can tell the big ones from the little ones, honey. *I'll* do the sorting."

"The dogs do all the work." She studied her coffee for a moment, and he waited for the second shoe to drop. "Tate, I know it's just an expression, but I think it would be better if you'd try not to use it, um . . . in this particular case."

"What expression?" He was truly at a loss. If he'd said a cuss word, it had slipped right out without him even hearing it.

"Honey."

Honey was bad? "Just an expression," he agreed.

"Jody might hear it and get the wrong impression."

"Which is—" he gave her the opening, but she left it to him to fill in the blank "—that maybe I like you some?"

"*Some?*" Her indulgent smile rankled *some*. "Jody wouldn't understand that 'honey' just means 'female' to you."

"So I should use the word *female?*" He tried it out. "I can tell the ewes from the lambs, *female?* Or should I say, I can tell the females from the kids? But kids are goats," he amended with a boyish grin. Now that he was rolling, he had her rocking with laughter. "If I start calling the ewes 'honey,' I want you to get me to a shrink, right away. Sign the commitment papers and tell 'em I'm crazy as a sheepherder."

"Crazy as a pregnant *female* sheepherder?"

"Uh-uh." He shook his head slowly, enjoying the sparkle in her big brown eyes. "Just 'crazy as a sheepherder.' It's a cowboy expression. You've got a *cowboy* workin' for you, lady. You can boss his hands, but not his mouth."

"First *ma'am,* then *honey,* and now it's *lady.* I don't know." Her laughter dwindled into a sigh. "They say cowboys are just naturally fickle."

"Can't live with 'em, can't shoot 'em."

"Can't resist 'em, either," she mumbled, drowning the better part of the comment in her coffee cup.

"What was that?" Had he heard her right? With a quick shake of her head, she jumped up from the table, leaving him to guess whether his ears had lied to him.

He shrugged and let it go. "Anyway, what I was trying to say was, I've got a pretty good whistle on me. I can do the sorting. I don't want you out there in those pens until you've calved out."

She returned with the coffeepot and poured him a refill. "Wet your whistle with this, cowboy. You'll need it. It's hard to get the dogs to work for somebody they're not used to. They're my dogs, and they're my pens and I'm not a cripple. I'm just—"

"The mule-headedest woman I ever met. You can supervise, okay? Give orders." His fork clattered on the plate as he took a swipe at his mouth with a paper napkin. "To the dogs, not me. You can tell me what to do, but not how to do it. I might be herdin' your damn sheep, but I've still got some pride left."

"I never doubted that." She smiled complacently as she claimed his empty plate.

He sighed. "So how many head are we sellin'?"

"I sold half the crop as spring lambs back in July, but the price wasn't nearly what I needed to get, so I've been holding off on the balance to put more weight on them." She let her guard down and eyed him solemnly. "I'm running out of time, though."

"They're not spring lambs anymore."

"No, but they're still lambs. Nice ones. They're pretty and plump right now. I was betting on a friendlier fall market, but it hasn't improved much, and my bills need to be paid. I think I'll be able to meet them. I really think I will." She was working hard to convince somebody, but he didn't think it was him.

"Did Ken have any insurance?" Tate asked. Without looking him in the eye, she shook her head. It surprised him a little, but he didn't let it show, because it would have embarrassed her.

"Insurance premiums aren't at the top of the priority list when you've got your whole life ahead of you, and your whole life is tied up in this place."

"Kenny inherited this place."

"And we mortgaged it to stock it and buy equipment. The land and the house. That was Ken's share. The rest was up to him." She slipped the plate into a sink full of soapy water. "When he married me, it was up to *us*."

Tate snagged a toothpick from the little red container that stood next to the pepper shaker. "But he's gone now, and *us* adds up to you and a little—*two* little kids." He slid his chair back from the table.

"It's the life I want for me and my two little kids. So I'm going to fight for it."

"Then I guess I'd better saddle up and move some sheep." He ambled over to the counter, thinking a toothpick was a poor substitute for a cigarette, but a guy had to make do. "Speaking of priority lists, I fixed the shower."

"Already?"

"Didn't take a lot of study, just a little muscle. You tell me what needs doing, and I'll figure out how to do it." He drained the last of his coffee before he handed her the mug. "But if you don't clue me in on the rest of your list, I'll have to come up with one on my own."

"See if you can get the dogs to go with you." She made it sound like a consolation of some kind. "Once you get them out in the pasture, they know what to do. Getting them to work the sheep in the pens takes a little more direction."

See if you can get the dogs to go with you. As if a sheepdog was going to be particular about keeping company with a cowboy. But when he let the two out of the kennel, they took off hell-bent-for-leather for the tall grass in the shelter belt. An explosive beating of pheasant wings promptly had them yapping their fool heads off as a ring-necked cock sailed majestically out of reach, his coppery feathers stealing a glint of sunrise.

"Nice move, bird," Tate said, turning a squint-eyed grin up to the sky. "To listen to *her* talk, you'd think these two sheepdogs had more brains than a cattleman." He plucked the toothpick from the corner of his mouth and tucked his tongue against his teeth, but then thought better of giving a whistle so close to little Jody's bedroom window. He used the toothpick as a pointer. "Come on, you two, we've got work to do."

All they did was play around. They chased each other around the shed while Tate gathered up his gear. They spooked the buckskin while Tate was trying to get him to take the bit. Damn horse was head-shy as it was. The rowels on Tate's spurs jingled as he gave a hop into the stirrup and swung into the saddle. The dogs ran circles around him as he trotted past the yard-light pole.

"If you two mutts are goin' with me, you can stop actin' like jackrabbits any time now."

"The collie's name is Duke, and the spotted bitch is Daisy," Amy called out. "She's a Catahoula Leopard."

Tate hadn't heard the door open, but there she was, waving to him from the back porch like he was some kind of explorer heading out to sea. "I can see that," he called back.

"She's won two blue ribbons."

"For what? Chasing cars?"

"They know their names." As showy as the pheasant's feathers, Amy's rich chestnut hair trapped a red glint of sunlight. She gave another jaunty wave. "Just call them."

He didn't need her advice on what to call them. "Come on, you fleabags. We're burnin' daylight."

When he topped the rise, he looked back. The dogs had treed some varmint, and their tongues were lolling in apparent expectation that the thing would fall out of the branches and land at their feet. One more chance was all they were going to get.

Tate popped a crisp whistle. "Daisy! Duke! Get your carcasses up here!"

And they came a-running.

The dogs had pushed the sheep along the draws without much coaxing from Tate, but it was a wonder to watch them work the pens for Amy. She whistled like nine different kinds of bird and used hand signals to let the dogs know which animals to drive where. All Tate and Jody had to do was mind the gates.

He still didn't like the idea of letting her get near any livestock so close to her time. Sheep had legs. They could kick. She was already getting kicked pretty good on the inside. When she paused to rub the side of her belly, he whacked the gate shut on the pen where he was working and started to go to her, but then she smiled. Another one of those little kicks. He clenched his fists to stop himself from going to her anyway and putting his hand where hers was. He liked feeling the movement inside her. It was sort of like having a new foal trust him enough to come close and nuzzle his palm, then stand still for a little friendly petting.

"What time are they sending the truck?"

"Five," she told him. "I want to be at the sale barn when they're unloaded so that I can get them settled down and fed."

"You're staying right here." With a quick gesture he cut off her protest as he strode across the corral, closing in on her. "Look at you. You're all done in. If you

wanna go to the sale tomorrow and have your remarkable business-lady wits about you, you'll let
me…" He heard footsteps tagging along behind him,
at least three steps to his one. Without missing a beat,
he scooped Jody up in his arms and patted the back
pockets of his pint-size blue-jeans. "You'll let *Jody
and me* take care of the grunt work tonight. Right,
partner? You think we can handle it?"

Jody nodded vigorously.

"I'm not a business *lady*. I'm a business…"

"Person. Female. Female person. Give me a break,
Amy. I got the remarkable part right, didn't I? And
I'm just trying to give *you* a break." As part of the
effort, he held the gate open for her. "I suggest you
take me up on it. It would be downright humiliating
if you happened to collapse at the sale barn and I had
to carry you out of there. I mean, what if I couldn't lift
you?"

She laughed and shook her head as she headed for
the house.

"Huh? What if I had to haul you out in a wheel-
barrow?" Close on her heels, Tate gave Jody a male-
conspiratory wink. "How much does a pregnant lady
weigh, anyway? Pregnant *female,* pardon me."

"I *do* think of myself as a lady, but not like, 'Whoa,
that's too much for you to handle, *little lady.* Better let
a *man* take over for you.'"

"Did I say that? Hey, I've made my reputation as a
top hand. You're a *sheep* rancher. You think I'd set my
sights on takin' over for a sheep rancher? No, ma'am.
Not this cowboy. I'll just be Miz Becker's hired hand,

down on his luck and workin' for a dollar a day and board. Only way to hang on to my self-respect."

"A dollar a day?" At the top of the back steps she turned to him, hands on her hips, and flashed a saucy smile. "When did I give you a raise?"

Amy's lambs did better than most, but prices were depressed. So was Amy. She didn't say a word on the way home from the auction. There wasn't much supper conversation, either, and anything coming from Amy was directed quietly at Jody. Tate felt like an interloper. He helped Jody clear the table. When the boy was told it was his bath time, Tate figured he'd been dismissed from the domestic scene. He went downstairs, flopped back on his bunk and played a few tunes he'd taught himself over the years on the harmonica he'd gotten from his dad. His *real* dad. He thought of him as Carter Harrison, the black-and-white photo phantom. Carter had played the harmonica, too. Sad songs, his mother had told him. Songs to fit his mood, like, "I'm So Lonesome I Could Cry."

"Can you teach me to play that?"

Tate raised his head and smiled. Jody looked small and wide-eyed and shy, standing there in his blue pajamas with the plastic-soled feet. Eagerly awaiting his cue, he gripped the door frame, ready to pop in or vanish, depending on Tate's answer.

"I can try," Tate offered.

Jody fairly leapt across the threshold, skidding to a stop at Tate's knee.

"How much time do we have before you have to be in bed?" The boy managed to shrug his shoulders as high as his ears, but Tate detected a guilty look in his eyes, which probably meant he was supposed to be in bed already. He decided to risk it. "I'd say we've got some time."

The two sat side by side on the narrow bed. Tate tapped the harmonica in his palm a few times, then held it steady for Jody and directed him through a series of notes. "Now the same thing, only a little faster," Tate said, and Jody complied intently. "What song did you play?" Tate asked at the end.

Jody gave a big-eyed smile, his blond curls shimmering under the overhead light. "'Twinkle, Twinkle Little Star.'"

"That's right. Did you know that's a cowboy's song?" Jody shook his head. "Sure is. You're camped out under the stars, you got your saddle for a pillow, your ol' six-shooter handy in case you find a rattler in your bedroll."

Jody's eyes grew big as saucers as Tate animated his tale with broad gestures.

"You take out your mouth organ, and you serenade the stars. This is their theme song." He slid the instrument back and forth across his lips and played the familiar tune again. "They like that all over, and, man, do they twinkle in that big Montana sky."

"Let me do it again."

By the time Jody returned the instrument, Tate was ready to pay him to stop twinkling. They shared a pillow while Tate played every soft, soothing song he knew. Jody finally drifted off to sleep. Tate carried him upstairs and managed to sneak past Amy's room. The desk light was on, and her back was to the door. He figured she was going over the books, dividing the amount of the lamb check among the outstanding bills. She'd been at it awhile. Either she had an extremely long column of numbers, or the check just wasn't big enough.

He decided to take her a comfort offering, and he knew she liked tea. He wanted to let her know that he didn't have to be told what her problems were. He'd been around long enough to take account. He had some ideas, and when she rejected those out of hand, as she was bound to do, he would be prepared with some alternatives. She was a fighter with her back to the wall. She would probably take a swing at him out of frustration, but he was pretty good at ducking. He could also be pretty good at talking sense. And because she was basically a sensible woman, eventually she would hear him out.

But she'd fallen asleep over her books. He stood in the doorway, steaming cup in hand, trying to decide whether he should knock or just walk right in like he owned the place. He wasn't going to leave her slumped over the desk for the night.

She solved his problem by awakening with a start, as though someone had shouted in her ear. She gripped the edge of the little writing desk and turned on him abruptly, her chair swiveling like the lid of a mayonnaise jar. He was sure he hadn't made a sound. Impatiently she swept the mop of errant hair out of her face and, with an indignant look, challenged him to explain himself.

He lifted the cup. "Tea."

She gave him a blank stare.

He was tempted to turn on his heel and leave her to sleep sitting up if it pleased her, but he said, "I thought I could get you to take a break, but I see..."

"For me?"

"Well, yeah. If I'd made it for me, I'd 'a put a kick in it." He sniffed the steam. "Smells like virgin orange."

She smiled. Finally. "What is a *virgin* orange?"

"Pure." He circled the foot of the bed and offered her the cup. "I read the box. It's got some kind of natural sleeping potion in it, but you have to be in bed for it to work."

"It doesn't say you have to be in bed."

"*You* have to be in bed—" he checked his watch as he sat down on the bed "—by midnight, so put the books away. Can I sit here?"

"You've already made your wrinkles in my coverlet." Flustered, he started to get up again. "Just kidding," she said quickly. "I'm not *that* fussy." She sipped the hot tea, then puzzled over it. "I do have to wonder why you're being so nice to me."

"Why wouldn't I be?" he asked, then added with mock indignation, "What, I don't have it in me to be nice?"

"You have it in you to be...a lot of things, I'm sure."

"Versatility is my stock in trade. I like being a lot of things. Keeps life interesting." He sat spraddle-legged, hands braced on his knees. "But I'm between jobs right now. It's either hire on to push an eighteen-wheeler down the road for a while, or tend sheep. Never had much truck with sheep."

He chuckled at his own wit and caught the weary smile in her eyes, peering at him above the rim of her cup.

"Guess it's something different," he allowed. "Besides, I'll take the view from the back of a horse over a truck cab, any day. Even if it's a view of sheep rumps headin' home."

"I'd like to get rid of the horses. All of them. Especially that outlaw you brought back here."

"One thing I can tell you for sure, Amy. It wasn't ol' Outlaw's fault." He paused for her objection, but she only drank more tea. "I figure he must be the one Kenny was riding that night. He's high-lifed, but he's a good horse. If he got spooked or missed his footing..." She gave him a sharp look, and he added quietly, "Kenny would be the first to tell you not to blame the horse."

"You're saying he shouldn't have been out riding that night."

"I'm saying it happened, and there's no sense to it. It's the kind of thing that could happen to anyone. Kenny drew the wrong cards that night."

"He shouldn't have been playing cards," she said flatly. "Or drinking. Or riding out there by himself. Or—" Quiet anger rose in her voice, and there was only Tate to be angry with.

"That was Kenny." Her husband, his friend, but they'd both known the same man. "He was a good-hearted, easygoin' guy who didn't like to think too far ahead."

"Well, I *do* think ahead." She was staring so hard at the papers on her desk that he half expected to see the edges start curling up and smoking. "I plan things. I planned the way I was going to sell the lambs, and I planned on getting more for them. Now I'll have to sell breeding stock so I can buy feed."

"I've been giving that some thought," he said lazily as he folded his hands behind his head and leaned back against her brass headboard. "I know I'm not getting paid to do any thinkin', but, hell, it just happens sometimes. You didn't take any hay off my land this year."

"We hadn't paid the lease." Her eyes darted about the room, finding bits of her explanation in every corner of the room, anywhere except in his eyes. "I didn't have anyone to cut it, anyway. Not that I would have, without your... I know Kenny agreed to cut it on shares, and then... I should have let you know that wasn't happening, so you could have made a deal with someone else, but—" She resigned herself with a long sigh. "I'm sorry. That was irresponsible of me."

"Well, now that you've got that off your chest, you can forget about it, okay? I'm not hurtin' for crop money or lease money or any of that. Come spring, I'll see about selling the land." With a gesture he dismissed the whole issue. He was eager to put forth his plan. "I figure with a little supplement we can put the herd out there and graze them 'til it gets too cold. Meanwhile, I'll shop around for some hay."

"I can't buy hay," she informed him stiffly. "I don't have the money."

"What if I said that I do?" She didn't need to say anything, what with that granite look in her eyes. "Yeah, that's what I thought."

"I should just sell those worthless horses."

"Now, I wouldn't call them worthless. They've got potential." He ignored her delicate sneer. "But if you sold them now, they'd go for killers. Butcher meat and dog food's about the only market for unbroke horses right now."

"They're registered quarter horses."

"And we both know that doesn't matter. Stock prices are low across the board. Nobody's got money for horses right now."

"Ken did." The resentment in her voice did battle with the guilt in her eyes. "He always had money for another great horse bargain."

"That's because he had you, makin' ends meet." Guilt gave way to a flash of gratitude. He understood. He smiled sympathetically. "So now you're done buying horses, and you've sold your lambs, and you're down to your ace-in-the-hole."

"Which is?"

"You've found yourself some cheap labor. You let him do what he can for you."

She looked at him, long and hard, and he could almost hear those gears clicking away inside her head, questioning, always trying to figure the odds and hedge her bets. In her position, he couldn't blame her.

"Why?" she asked finally.

"Because you're a smart woman, Amy. And you've run low on options."

"I mean, why are you willing to do this?"

"It's kinda out of character, isn't it?" He smiled knowingly. "I don't like being too predictable. Every once in a while I like to be nice. I like to be useful to somebody, just for a change."

"I never said you weren't nice . . . sometimes."

"Boy, that was a squeaker." He laughed and shook his head as he got up to leave. "On that happy note and the strike of the eleventh hour, I'd better drag my tail downstairs."

"I know *I'm* not always nice," she admitted with another sigh. "I didn't even thank you for the tea." She took another drink, just to show him that she wasn't going to let it go to waste. He figured it had to be cold by now. "This is nice, and I thank you."

"My pleasure." He touched her shoulder as he passed. Her surprisingly unguarded look of appreciation made him want to hang around the bedroom a little longer. "I fed the ewes. Tomorrow morning I'll start moving some grain feeders out to my place. I'll be putting the rams out there with them." She raised one brow, but he detected the hint of a smile. "Won't I? I mean, is that your plan, boss lady?"

"We'll have to watch the weather closely if we're going to move them over to your place."

"This is Montana." He chuckled. "What else have we got to do in the winter?"

"Some of the grain feeders might need a little repair," she warned.

"I've already got that covered." He gave her a reassuring wink as he turned to leave.

"Tate?" He glanced over his shoulder, eyebrows raised. "I may not always be nice, either, but I *am*

good. I try to be a good person, anyway. I do understand why you're doing all this. I know how you felt
about Ken, and I don't want to take advantage of you,
especially since I didn't make much of an effort to—"

"If you're seeing some advantage to be taken, I'm
makin' progress."

It took him a good part of the morning to make the
repairs on the free-standing grain feeders and put them
in accessible locations. When he came back he found
his lunch waiting for him, but the house was deserted. Jody was playing with a fleet of toy trucks
outside the barn, and Amy was inside, sitting in a pile
of straw with the shoulders of a one-hundred-and-
seventy-pound ewe planted in her lap.

"What the hell do you think you're doing?"

"Poor baby had a nail in her hoof."

Hunkering down next to her, he pulled off one
buckskin work glove, pushed her open coat aside and
laid his hand protectively over her belly. "*This* is a
baby," he corrected, and with a gloved finger he
touched the ewe's foot. "This, as you know, is a hoof.
This hoof might kick this baby."

"The hoof belongs to a sheep, not a horse or a cow.
They have to be trimmed every fall," she explained as
she continued to pare the cloven hoof. "And since
we're going to move them, I have to get them all
done."

"God—*bless*, woman!" The docile, flop-eared ewe
sniffed at his jacket, but she was no more intimidated
by his exasperated protests than Amy was. Ordinarily
he wasn't one to expound much, but he figured a les-

son was in order. "A hoof is a hoof." End of chapter one. He sat down on Amy's straw cushion. "Why don't you tell me about these things before you go and—"

"I *always* trim their hooves, twice a year, and I have never gotten hurt doing it. They're gentle animals, Tate."

"Tell that to the two rams I just separated."

"Well, the rams..." She inspected the inner hoof for debris, probing with her parer. "They do butt heads during breeding season. It's a man thing." She spared him a coy glance. "I'll let you take care of the rams."

"I'll tell you something else that's a man thing." He draped his forearms over his knees and removed his other glove. "You see a woman in your condition, you just wanna put her in a pumpkin shell and keep her very well until everything's—" he slapped his palm with the leather glove "—over with. Safe and sound."

"And a woman in my condition happens to have a good deal of energy, especially as the time draws closer. She wants to make sure everything is in order, and nature seems to provide her with the energy to do just that." She looked up at him. "I couldn't breathe in a pumpkin shell. You need your space, Tate. Let me have mine."

"I'll let you show me how to do this," he offered as he scooted the ewe from her lap to his. A hoof was a hoof, he'd said, and he'd trimmed his share. He held his hand out for the knife.

"Actually, I was going to need some help catching them. This one was limping, so she was slower than I was." She relinquished the tool to him. It was useless to argue, and she knew he didn't need much instruction. "I'm used to handling most of it myself, but Jody's helping out, too, now. He can bottle-feed a lamb. He can—"

"Jody's just a little guy." Too young to be given some of the jobs he kept asking for. Tate remembered how it felt to be given the kind of responsibility that made a boy feel like a man. Heady at first, but there was no turning back once you'd taken the step. At least there hadn't been for him.

"I heard you reading that nursery rhyme to him the other night, about the pumpkin shell," he said. It was the kind of kids' stuff he'd sailed right past on his shortcut to manhood. "What's that supposed to mean, 'had a wife but couldn't keep her'? You don't get married unless you've got some way to keep her."

"Keep her what?" Amy teased. "Happy? It's usually the woman's lament, that she had a husband but couldn't keep him."

"Keep him what?" he echoed.

They traded smiles while he switched to the other front hoof. Then he made short work of the back hooves and let the animal go.

"When are you going to settle down?" she wondered. "For longer than a few months, I mean."

"The word *when* supposes I will, sooner or later." The straw rustled beneath him as he shifted, raising his knee for an armrest. "Is that what you suppose? Every man oughta settle down, sooner or later?"

"They don't all want to. I know that. And some try to have it both ways." He looked up, wordlessly asking whether she meant him. "Ken wasn't like that." Missing Tate's message, she went on. "He had built-in roots. I like that. I found a sense of security in it. That's funny, isn't it?"

"Why?" He felt no urge to laugh now that she'd changed the subject to Kenny's attributes.

"Because he found a way to wander off after all, didn't he?" It wasn't the answer he was ready for, nor the one she'd expected to give. She glanced away quickly. "I don't know why I said that. It's a terrible thing to say."

"But it's true. He's gone, and you're still here."

"He didn't mean to," she said sadly as she picked a piece of straw off his thigh. "He never meant to leave us. He didn't even know he was leaving *two* children, and he didn't mean for things to be so—" Here it comes, he thought. He couldn't see her eyes, but her voice was weakening. "—damn hard."

"It's okay." She shook her head as he took her hands in his. "No, come on, Amy, it's okay to tell it like it is."

"It isn't like that. He's not to blame." She glanced at the open barn door, her eyes shining with the threat of tears. "That horse, that crazy horse."

"I'll get rid of the horse," he promised. Her bottom lip trembled, but she said neither aye nor nay. Gently he squeezed her hands. "Will that help?"

"Yes!" She closed her eyes and shook her head again as he moved into position. "No, no, no, it won't do any good."

"Come here, honey." He reached out to her, ready to hold her, anticipating the feel of her weight against him. "It'll do you good to—"

"No," she said firmly, wiping her eyes with one hand and pushing him away with the other. Jody's truck-engine sound effects intruded from a distance. "I can't let Jody see me like this."

"Why not?"

"I'm all he's got." She scrambled to her feet so fast that he missed his chance to offer any gentlemanly assistance. "And I can't come apart now. I don't have time. I have too much to do. I have to—" Her hands were shaking as she struggled for control. "*We* have to get those hooves trimmed."

She'd streaked some dirt across her cheek with the tear she'd banished so quickly. He reached his hand out to her. "Amy, take it easy." He would clean her face if she would let him. He would kiss away her tears.

"Are you going to help me or not?"

Her lips were trembling, and her eyes were wild with an emotion he couldn't begin to name. He let his hand fall to his side. "I'm gonna do the work," he said gruffly. "You give the damn orders."

Chapter Four

In trade for hay, Tate agreed to break a couple of two-year-olds for Myron Olson. He knew Myron needed green-broke two-year-olds about as much as he needed a swimming pool in his backyard this winter, but Myron happened to have plenty of hay and welcomed the excuse to truck some over to the Becker place. Like some of the other neighbors, he'd offered to help the widow out with whatever she needed, but she always said she was doing just fine.

Just what she needed, Amy grumbled when he unloaded the new stock. More horses around the place. But Tate detected a glint of relief in her eyes when the first load of hay rolled into the yard. He wasn't going to let the horses interfere with his other chores, but he liked to work with them when he was minding Jody, who loved to watch. Tate found himself wishing Amy would come out to observe him in action, too, just to reassure herself that it was perfectly safe to keep horses around.

"Mama, Mama, Mama!"

Jody only called her "Mama" when he was excited or scared. The way his little legs were churning up the gravel, she could tell he was both. She flew out the door and met him at the foot of the back steps.

"Come quick! Tate got kicked!"

"Where!"

"In the head, by one of the—"

She took his hand, and together they trotted across the yard. "Show me where."

"It's nothing," Tate insisted as soon as Amy and Jody burst into the barn. He was sitting on a hay bale, hat in one hand, head in the other, looking like a guy who'd just lost round one. "I'm okay. Just grazed me. No blood spilled." But when he took his hand away from his forehead, he had a glove full of blood. "*Hardly* any blood spilled."

"You're bleeding all over the place!" Amy exclaimed as she knelt beside him, trying to catch her breath. "Can you walk?"

"Legs are fine." He scowled, arching the eyebrow that was catching most of the blood. "You been running?"

"Jody's been running. I've been waddling."

"You shouldn't be running." He took a swipe at the blood with the back of his wrist as he tried to duck away from her scrutiny.

"*You* shouldn't be—" She took his face in her hands and made him look at her. The light was dim, and his eyes were so dark that it was hard to tell anything about his pupils. "Can you walk?"

"You asked me that." He proved he could stand up. "Point me in the right direction."

"You okay, Tate?" Jody asked anxiously.

"If I start to go down, just holler 'Timber!' and get your mom out of the way."

"That's not funny," Amy insisted as she slipped her arm around him. He put his arm around her shoulders, and she gave his flat belly a motherly pat as they headed for the house. "You'll be okay."

"That's what I said. Just feelin' a little booze blind, which is no big deal." But he grabbed for the gatepost as they entered the yard, taking a moment to steady himself without leaning on her. "Except you'd like to start out with some fun before you get the headache."

"You mean you're not having fun yet, cowboy? You and your damned hardheaded horses."

"I'm the hardhead." He closed his eyes briefly, then forced a smile. "The horses are jugheads. There's a difference."

"I'm sure I don't know what that is."

"The difference is, I should have known better. I was sackin' her out, and I should've used a hobble."

"We don't need the hay this bad," she said as Jody scampered up the steps and held the door for them.

"Yes, we do." Neither of them had accented the word *we*, but it resounded in the look they exchanged. "And it's not bad," he assured her quietly. "I'd know if it was bad. I've been kicked before."

"I don't like taking charity."

"It's hardly charity when I'm . . ." He was looking for a place to sit before he collapsed. She provided a tall kitchen stool close to the sink, and he sank down on it gratefully. "I'm working for the damn hay, and I'm doing it on your time."

"Stop patronizing me. I'm not paying you, and even if I were, I wouldn't pay you to get kicked in the head by a horse."

"I'll get the doctoring stuff," Jody offered sensibly. He disappeared down the hall.

Amy grumbled as she set to work on Tate's head with a clean towel, soap and water. "I don't want anyone else getting hurt. Horses are dangerous, they're unpredictable, they're . . ." She worked gently around the cut, brushing his hair back with one hand and blotting the blood with the other. "Tate, this won't stop bleeding. You probably need stitches."

"If you say so." He almost lost himself in the sympathy he saw in her eyes, but Jody's return brought him back to reality. A bottle and two small boxes clattered on the counter. Tate rewarded the boy with a smile. "We'll go get us some stitches. Right, Jody?"

"You mean you can sew his head?"

"I can't," Amy said absently, still trying to staunch the blood. "A doctor can."

"Will it hurt?" Jody backed away slowly. Remembered fear crept into his question. "Is it like an operation? Will he die?"

"Jody, come here." Tate held out his hand. "It's not like an operation, and I'm going to be fine."

"You didn't fall off a horse, did you?" Jody asked anxiously, inching closer.

Tate shook his head as he hooked his hand around the boy's nape and drew him close.

"No," Jody reassured himself. He draped himself over Tate's thigh as though he were hitching a ride. "You got kicked, but you never fell off. That's different."

"I've fallen off lots of horses," Tate admitted, looking to Amy for approval. He was willing to admit to the risks. "Sometimes you get hurt, but most of the time you just dust off your jeans and climb back on."

"Or you get smart and stay away from them because they're dangerous," she instructed as she peeled adhesive tape from a roll. "Jody knows that."

Tate ruffled Jody's soft curls. "I'm okay, Jody. In a week or so, this will just look like a scratch."

"And don't tell him it doesn't hurt, either, because it does." She sucked air between her teeth, grimacing as she considered the best way to cover the wound. Finally she bit the bullet and applied the bandage. Tate winced. "I'm sorry. Does that hurt?"

"It does hurt a little. You'd probably feel a lot better if I took some aspirin or something."

"We're taking you in for some stitches, and then I want those horses—" She swept them away with a quick gesture.

"Uh-uh." Tate wagged his index finger under her nose. "I took on a job, and I'll get it done. But I'll be more careful."

"You could sue me, and I don't have any liability insurance," she suggested too easily. His steely, dispassionate look set her back on her heels. "I guess you wouldn't sue me."

"I guess I hadn't thought of it."

"I did have insurance, but I didn't pay the premium this fall. That's the next thing on my list, but I haven't had . . ."

"Jody," Tate began, giving the boy a pat on the back. "Just between us, I don't feel much like driving the pickup. You wanna go look in your mom's sewing box and find me a needle and a piece of thread about—" he thrust his white shirtsleeve in front of Jody's face "—this shade of passin'-out pale?"

Amy threw in the towel. "I'm getting my coat."

A few hours of convalescing went a long way with Tate. And a little TLC was about all Amy had the time for. Otherwise, about the only progress he could say he'd made with her in the time that he'd worked for her was that she didn't seem to hate him. He wasn't sure what more he wanted from her. Not sex, obviously; she wasn't exactly in any shape for a real good roll in the sack. Maybe a little cuddling in the sack, where he could hold her close enough to feel the baby move again.

Hell, what was he thinking? It wasn't even his baby, and she damn sure wasn't his woman. He didn't know why he kept hanging around. She couldn't bring herself to admit she needed his help. If anybody asked, she was honest enough to admit she needed *some* help, but any damn drifter with a strong back would do, long as she kept her shotgun handy in case he had any ideas about . . .

In case he had the nerve to think about getting her in the sack, where she could put her hands on him the way she had when he'd been hurt. She was the kind of woman who might reject a man's appetite for the roving and rollicking life, but she could still touch him with forgiving, healing, caring hands. Maybe if she would once touch him in the dark, he thought. Maybe if they couldn't see into each other's eyes, they wouldn't be as likely to start the delicious drowning, start the lovely slipping under, then, bam! There was Kenny, floating above their heads like an avenging angel.

And Amy would end up feeling bad about spending any of her affection on Tate. She'd felt bad about it years ago, even before she'd married Kenny, and it would be worse for her now that he was dead. She was too damn hard on herself. She wouldn't think it was a good thing for a good woman to do, and she was good. She had certain standards she tried to live by. She'd made a point of reminding him of that. It wasn't just a matter of being good at what she did. Hell, *he* was good at what he did, not that what he did was any great shakes, but he was good at it. Still, he wasn't *good*.

And just to prove it, he was about to do Saturday night up right.

He started out at the Jackalope, but the atmosphere was too dismal there. Charlie Dennison had gotten his butt in a sling at home. His ol' lady had thrown all his gear into a cardboard box and left it on the back porch. No question that ol' Charlie was completely misunderstood. That put Ticker Thomas in mind of the girl he should have married, damn sure *would* have married if she hadn't run off to Seattle. The music was downhearted, the drinking was solemn and the patrons were all male.

After one drink Tate moved on to the Turkey Track, where the dance floor was hopping. He met up with Kenny's sister, Marianne, who had managed to persuade husband Bill, Sr., Overo's staid, colorless grocer, to shock everybody by taking his wife out on a Saturday night. Marianne professed to be damn glad to see Tate and damn sorry she hadn't tried to get hold of him herself when Kenny died. She'd just assumed—well, everybody knew Tate was footloose.

"You remember Patsy Drexel. Used to be Johnson," Marianne shouted over the strains of "The Devil Went Down to Georgia." She shoved the voluptuous blonde into his arms, and he took a turn around the dance floor with her.

Sure, he remembered Patsy. Patsy was Marianne's friend. Three years ahead of him in school and lightyears ahead of him in experience, at least to start out with. Experience had been one hell of a zealous teacher. They'd had some good times together back then, and once or twice in the intervening years, whenever he'd happened to be in town and Patsy had happened to be between husbands.

"Drexel," he said consideringly. That was a new one. "So you got married again, huh?" Before the conversation went the way it usually did with Patsy, he had to get a few things straight. "Where's your ol' man?"

"Which one? The last one ran off to Reno to play guitar in a band. He had the hots for the singer." She looked up and smiled. "It was an even shorter marriage than my first. You think I oughta take back my maiden name now that I'm unattached again?"

"I've still got you down as Johnson in my memory book. Is that your maiden name?" He charmed her with a wink. Here was opportunity tapping a bright red fingernail just above his shoulder blade.

But when he escorted her back to the table, she made the mistake of saying, "Thanks, honey." He wasn't sure where the prickly sensation had come from, but he told himself to ignore it.

"So you're working out to Becker's place for the winter?" Patsy claimed the chair next to Marianne's. "Haven't seen her around town for a while. Bet she's big as a hippo and twice as testy."

"She's all baby," Tate said tightly as he lit a cigarette. "She looks uncomfortable, but I don't hear her complaining."

He eyed Patsy pointedly as he blew a stream of smoke, hoping she'd gotten the message that bad-mouthing Amy wouldn't earn her any points with him, if that was what she was looking for. Patsy was in no position to talk, anyway. From what he could see, all her experience had put more age on her than any UV rays could account for.

"Well, it's real nice of you to help her out," Patsy allowed generously. "But it must be frustrating in a way, considering how you've always kinda carried a torch for her."

"What are you talking about? Amy's the vine-covered cottage type, and I've never been one to let any grass grow under my feet." There, he thought, that sounded definite. "Besides, she was a one-man woman, and that man was my best friend." For good measure he mentally toasted Kenny before he took a drink.

"You might've been hiding your torch under a bush, Tate, but everyone knew it was there. That's why you left Overo."

He smiled humorlessly as he aligned his glass with the water ring it had left on the table. "I had a lot of reasons for leaving Overo, and Amy Becker wasn't one of them."

"You walked away from your father's land," Marianne said. "That place was rightfully yours, not your stepfather's, from the day your mother died. It was always Harrison land."

"It still is." He glanced at Bill, who was busy people-watching, then at Marianne. Patsy was the woman after his body, but Marianne was a woman after his own heart. Calculating and practical. Cut to the payoff. He just needed to put his basic instincts to work for a change. "Until somebody makes me a good offer."

"Check with some of the oil companies," Marianne advised. "There are about half a dozen speculators looking to take core samples, but some of these old ranchers around here refuse to poke anything but a posthole through the sod. And you know damn well there's money down there somewhere.''

Patsy leaned closer. "I can't see you as the sentimental type when it comes to poking holes wherever it suits you, Tate.'' Her smile was as suggestive as the beat of the music. "Whenever there's a need.''

"Leave it to a woman to fancy she can see right through a man's skin,'' he said smoothly.

"It's in your eyes, sugar. You've got a need.''

"Just a simple itch, honey.'' *Honey.* Damn. He adjusted the brim of his hat, which covered his bandage even while it punished him with a dull headache. He signaled the server for another round of drinks. "Alcohol works wonders.''

"Where does it itch? I just had a manicure.'' Patsy ran her nails up and down his back. "How does that feel? Tell me when I hit on the spot that's bothering you, sugar.'' Smiling lasciviously, she discovered her favorite thigh. "Am I getting warm?''

"You aren't even close, Patsy.'' He couldn't believe he was actually moving her hand, patting it apologetically as he settled it in her own lap. Damn his eyes, maybe he *was* getting sentimental in his old age, but he didn't feel much like poking around Patsy or vice versa. "Even if you were, it'd be no use. The itch just keeps on coming back.''

"That's because *you* keep coming back.''

"So do you.'' He nodded across the table. "So do *you*, Marianne. Remember when you lit out with that bull rider? Kenny and me had to do some fancy talkin' to keep your dad from headin' into Billings with a shotgun.''

"Those were my wilder days." Marianne turned to her husband, who was only half listening. "Can you believe I was ever that wild, honey?"

Bill, Sr., a dubious honey at best, responded with a grunt in the negative.

"We were all born to be wild," Patsy said, cheerfully resigning herself to Tate's rebuff. "That's how I look at it." Then she sang it, pounding on the table for added emphasis. "'Course, if *I* was born to be wild, what about my kids? God, I *dread* having teenagers."

"How many kids do you have?" Tate remembered hearing about one, but Patsy never talked about her children.

"Three. One for each of my two ex's, and one for this guy I used to work for. Thank God Sally's old enough to watch the other two once in a while."

"How old is she?" He was asking for the kind of details he'd always considered none of his business.

"Eleven," Patsy reported without the slightest show of emotion. "Almost twelve. Almost a teenager. Now *her* father was the one I should have kept around if I wanted to be married, but back then the grass looked greener in my boss's bed. Which it was for a while. Then I met the guitar player." She planted her elbow on the table and sank her chin into her hand. "One of these days I'm going to pack up and move to Denver."

"You think you'd like the grass down there better?"

"I don't know. I've just always wanted to live in Denver. Mile-high pie and all that."

"Denver's just like any other place," Tate said as the server appeared with a tray of drinks. "Take my word for it."

"The voice of experience," Patsy quipped sarcastically.

"That's right." Tate wanted to laugh, but he would be laughing *at* her, and he had no right. He was no better. In fact, she was his flip side. She had her experience, he had his.

"I suppose you've spent enough time there to really know."

"As much as I've spent anywhere." There was a dose of sympathy for each of them in his sad smile. "I really *do* know."

"Then you're lucky," Patsy insisted. "Do yourself a favor and don't settle down in any one spot for too long. Before you know it, things'll start to get sticky. You'll have all kinds of baggage and bills, ex-spouses and kids. That stickiness turns out to be glue, Tate. Before you know it—"

"For heaven's sake, Patsy, I try to fix you up with somebody, and you get morbid." Marianne's laughter lightened the mood. "If you can't have a good time with Tate Harrison, then you're over the hill, because, according to my brother, Tate always did know how to have a good time."

"I can vouch for Tate." Patsy gave him a wistful smile. "Even though it's been a long time."

"A long time for what?" Tate figured he could still party, even if he wasn't interested in finding somebody to take him home. "We were dancing just a minute ago."

"You're a great dancer."

"Well, then, let's dance." With a gallant flourish he assisted Patsy with her chair. "Let's just bop 'til we drop, and the hell with all the bills and the baggage."

It didn't do him a damn bit of good to tear up the dance floor with Patsy Johnson Drexel. The way she kept crowding him made slow dancing impossible. He favored a heel-kicking "Cotton-Eyed Joe" or a twirling "Cowboy Two-Step." When his eyes started playing tricks on him and blue-eyed Patsy suddenly went brown-eyed on him, he knew he was beyond dance-dizzy. He decided it was time to quit going through the motions and call it a night.

He was looking forward to falling into bed and spinning himself to sleep, although he realized as he shut off the pickup's engine that there wasn't much night left.

He found Amy standing in the middle of the kitchen, barefoot and dressed only in a pink cotton nightgown. She didn't seem to want to let go of the edge of the sink as she turned to him. Backlit by the light above the kitchen window, the curves of her fecund body made a lovely silhouette beneath the opaque gown. In that instant, Tate knew for certain that God was a woman. A man-God wouldn't have tortured him this way, like making him stand outside a bakery window during Lent.

"Are you just getting up, or just going to bed?" He didn't like the wounded-animal look in her eyes. He wanted to see fiery judgment, so he could say, *Back at you, baby*. But she just stood there while he hung his sheepskin jacket and his hat on the hooks in the back entry. "You weren't waiting up for me, were you?"

"Oh, no," she said quickly. She turned away from him as she tightened her grip on the edge of the sink. "I wouldn't do a foo—fooooolish thinglikethat."

"What's going on?" He crossed the floor in two strides and took her slight shoulders in his hands. "You okay?"

"I could use a top hand." Her shoulders were shaking. She struggled with words and shallow breaths. "You know of one who's not too...too busy? Oh, dear..."

"It's not time yet, is it?" Her whole body went stiff as she nodded vigorously. He pried her hand away from the sink and draped her arm over his shoulder. "We gotta sit you down. You mean, now?"

She pressed her face against his neck and let him lower her into a chair. His mind was spinning, but whiskey wasn't the cause. He'd never sobered up so fast in his life. One thing at a time, he told himself. "You hold on. I'll get you some clothes. I'll get Jody."

"I'm hoping he'll sleep."

"Sleep?" This was no time to argue with her, but it was definitely time to take charge. "Amy, we can't leave him here alone."

"I don't know about you, but I'm not going—" she held on to the seat of the chair as though she were preparing for a bumpy ride "—anywhere. Especially not with you driving."

"I got home all right, didn't I?" Damn right, he was home. *Home,* where he was needed, where it was all up to him now. "I can get you to—"

Her shoulders started to shake again as she dropped her head back. Holy God in heaven, he couldn't take her out on the road like this. The thing was, he had to stay calm. He had to do something quick, and it had to be the right thing. He laid his hand on her shoulder, and the phone on the wall caught his eye.

"You're right, honey. We'll call someone to— Amy!" She groaned softly and pressed the side of her face against his arm. He could feel her hurting. He felt like a powerless lump of male flesh, afraid to step away from her, scared to death not to.

"The first thing to do is get help." He took a step, reached for the phone, pointed a finger at the dial. "Who to call, who to call, who's close, nobody's close..."

"Tate." He hadn't heard her move, but she was leaning against his back now, her hands on his shoulders, just the way he had held her moments ago. "Tate, there's no one else right now. Just you."

"You mean it's coming right *now?* We have to tell them to come." He closed his eyes. His head was devoid of numbers. "Ambulance...police...what's the damn number for—"

"Right *here,* Tate." She laid her cheek against his back. He hung up the phone and turned to take her in his arms. "Having the baby...right here, right—"

"Not on the kitchen floor, honey, let's get you—" He lifted her easily as the answers started to come to him. Make her comfortable first, *then* call. "Okay, let's get you to bed, and I'll call—"

"I've called...the midwife...I've been seeing for prenatal exams. Left a message."

"Midwife? What is that, some sort of—"

"She'll be here." He laid her on her bed, which she'd apparently prepared in advance with a rubberized sheet. He wasn't sure what to make of all this, or of Amy's soft babbling. "Soon. She'll be here. It came on so f-fassst."

"What if..." A *midwife?* It sounded to him like something out of the Dark Ages. "I'm calling an ambulance."

"No," Amy insisted. She grabbed his arm and with amazing strength pulled him down close to her. "Now, listen to me, Tate, there's no time, and women have been having babies since time began, and they don't..."

He shook his head and tried to pull away, but even as another contraction started, she was having none of his resistance. "I don't have any health insurance, and I don't want any more bills I can't p-p—" She held his arm while he looked on in terror, gripping her shoulders. When it was over, she smiled bravely. "That was a good one."

"It didn't look good."

"Think of it as pulling...as calving out a...no, *easier* than a first-calf heifer, Tate. I'm on my second." Her eyes pleaded with him as she fought to control her breathing. "Tate, I'm afraid you're going to have to do this for me."

"Not me, for God's sake, I'm just as—" Just as what? Scared? Stupid? Weak-kneed as a new foal was the way he felt, but he tried to return that brave smile of hers. He brushed her damp hair back from her forehead. "I don't know anything about this, honey.

We need a doctor. Hell, if I make a mistake, you might sue me, like—"

"No, it's not funny. I have to be able to count on you. You have to deliver—"

"No, it's not safe. I might . . . Let me get you a doctor, honey. When the pain comes, let me just hold your hand until it—"

"Wash yours, damn it!" Then the pain seized her, along with all the anguish and frustration and anger that came with birthing. "Damn damn damn you, Tate! Look at me!"

"Hey, I wasn't anywhere near—" It didn't matter. The technicality wedged itself in his throat, and it occurred to him that there was no excuse for him. He was a man. Watching Amy suffer made him feel like a worm.

"I'm sorry, honey. I'm sorry." He smoothed her hair back again, kissed her hot temple and whispered, "Kenny's sorry, too."

"You smell like smoke—" She grabbed his hand and squeezed for all she was worth "—and beer, and you . . . and you . . . and you . . ."

"Shhhh, what can I do?"

"I don't wanna shhhh!"

"Yell, then, what can I do?"

"Oooh, oooh—" Pant. Pant. "I think you should wash your hands, and I put all the stuff Mrs. . . . midwife . . ." She waved her free hand toward the supplies she'd set out on a white towel on the dresser, then groaned. "Scissors and surgical thread . . . alcohol . . . Hurry, Tate, hurry—oooooh . . ."

Crossing the room in a single stride, Tate tore open his cuff and started rolling up his sleeve, but by the time he'd reached the bathroom sink, he'd stripped the shirt off entirely. He washed his hands and his arms up to his T-shirt sleeves. God help him, he was covered with germs and dirt and sin. He grabbed a bottle of rubbing alcohol and doused his hands in it. They seemed relatively steady, even though he felt like he'd swallowed a cement mixer.

"Tate!" Amy called, straining to control her voice. And then, "Taaaate!" She screamed his name as though things were coming apart and he was supposed to be able to put them back together. Like pulling a calf? *Pulling?* Oh, God, why did she have to say *that?* He took a deep breath and a big step.

"Tate!" Eyes wild with terror, Jody stood in the middle of the hallway. "Tate, my mama! Don't let my mama die, Tate!"

Chapter Five

"*My mom can't die of this, can she?*"

That had been Tate's question, too. Even in the best of times his stepfather had been a man of few words, but after his mother had gotten sick, no words had been forthcoming from Oakie Bain. No comfort. No counsel. Tate's questions went unanswered until the day Myron Olson's wife, Joan, had come to take him out of school. "Get your jacket," Joan had said, and he'd stared at the denim thing hanging on a coat hook in the hallway. It hadn't been washed since his mother had gone away to the hospital.

He remembered the sound of Joan's boots clopping down the hallway toward Jesse's classroom. There was his answer, in the sound of a woman's retreating footsteps. Never again would he hear the quiet voice that had willingly given him what answers she'd had. No more would he see the light of approval in his mother's eyes. The terrible reality had fallen over him like a weighted net. He'd felt hot-faced and sick to his stomach, and he'd barely made it to the boys' bathroom.

"Tate?" Jody's brown eyes were as big as basketballs.

Tate took a deep breath. "Your mom's having the baby. It's kinda like lambing. Have you seen a lamb get born?"

"Once," Jody said. "But Mama's screamin' a lot worse than a ewe."

"It hurts her pretty bad right now, but after the baby comes out, it'll stop hurting. It just takes a little while."

He knelt like a supplicant before the boy, holding his arms out awkwardly. "We're going to help her. I'm going to keep the door open, and you're going to sit right outside in the hallway and be ready to run and get me something if I need it, okay?"

Jody nodded hesitantly.

"We can't shake on it, because I have to keep my hands real clean, so put your arms around my neck and give me a hug." The little boy's arms gave him a shot of encouragement. His angel-hair curls clung to the stubble on Tate's jaw. "Thanks, partner."

Amy's breathy pain-ride suddenly sounded less threatening. Clear-eyed confidence took a firm grip on his insides. She needed him, and he was there. The rest would follow in due course.

She was between contractions.

"Do we need to anchor your legs somehow?"

She grimaced and shook her head.

He offered her a sympathetic smile. "Is this it, then? You gonna take this lyin' down, boss lady?"

She nodded again and lifted her chin, returning a tightly drawn, stiff-upper-lipped expression. "There's hardly any letup now." Her voice was stretched thin. "The pains are so bad...won't let me have an-nnnnunhhhh..."

She gripped the brass rails of the headboard as she gathered her forces at her middle. Her stamina amazed him. Unable to touch her, Tate stood watch over her labor.

Anxious eyes peered at him from the dim hallway. Jody was sitting there tight-lipped, clutching his knees, trusting Tate to do whatever needed to be done. Amy rolled her head to the side and saw him there. "Oh, Jody..." Her voice was weak, but her tone took exception to the child's presence.

"Jody's lookin' out for you, too," Tate said softly.

"But I don't want him to see me like thhhhhiii—"

Tate gave a nod. "Jody, I want you to stand guard right by the door, okay? Just like a soldier. And tell me if you hear anyone at the back door."

"Mama, are you gonna die?"

"No!" She turned her head away. "Oh no, oh no, oh no..."

Tate nodded again, and Jody scrambled for his assigned post on the other side of the doorjamb.

"He's scared, honey." He looked down into Amy's eyes, begging her indulgence. He knew she was up to it. He couldn't fathom the extent of her pain, but he could see how strong she was. "We can't shut him out. If you can just tell him you'll be okay..."

"I'm okay, Jody." She was getting hoarse. "I'm okay, I'mokayI'mokay—" She closed her eyes through the next contraction. A gush of water flooded the bed beneath her hips.

"Tate, I think it's time for you to—" Amy pulled her nightgown over her distended belly and spread her knees apart "—check...things...."

This was no time for modesty, and no time for him to back down from a woman's invitation to get personal. Not when a soggy thatch of baby hair was presenting itself at life's door. After the next contraction, Tate quickly swabbed Amy with rubbing alcohol. He'd barely managed to set the bottle aside when she gave a long, deep, terrible groan and pushed. Everything, including his eyes, widened. The tiny head was expelled.

"Good job, Amy!" He felt like a cheerleader in the playoffs—overstimulated and underuseful. "Can you do that again?"

"I can't *not* do it," she barked between gasps. "I can't—ohhhhh..."

"Mama?"

"She's doing fine," Tate said excitedly. His whole being was attuned to the sound of her doglike panting, the smell of life-producing blood and the sight of her body transforming itself in the most miraculous way. "You're doing great, honey. Just one more time."

"Jody, don't..."

"Jody, run get me some more towels," Tate ordered. Jody sprang from his post like a sprinter.

"Ohohohohoh..."

"And peek out the window to see if anyone's coming," Tate called out.

The baby's head turned to the side. Tate cleared its mouth with his big forefinger. Amy whimpered a little as she braced herself for the next onslaught. Tate braced himself against the sound of her pain, which erupted with a fury this time as the baby whooshed into Tate's waiting hands like a tot on a water slide. She bawled the minute he caught her.

"A little girl!"

She was all pink and petite and perfect, and he was actually holding her in his own two hands. A squirming, wrinkled female connected to her mother by a coiled cord, like the receiver on a telephone. Only *Tate* was the receiver. He bore the good news.

"Amy, she's here. Your little girl just made her debut."

"Is she okay?"

"Can't you hear her?" Grinning from ear to ear, he put the slippery prize on Amy's belly. Amy lifted her head, trying to get a peek. Her face was pale and slick with sweat. He took her cool hand in his slippery one and guided it to the baby's head. "She sounds just like you. All pretty and mad."

"Like me?" Chest heaving, Amy dropped her head back. "Not mad," she gasped. "Hardly pretty. But strong. I did it."

"Damn right, you did it. Hold on to her while I do the rest."

He hoped he was doing it right. In some ways it wasn't so different from the nonhuman births he'd attended. His hands were rock steady, and his heart was singing like a meadowlark as he snipped the cord between tiny tourniquets he'd made of surgical thread. "You're on your own now, little girl."

He was wrapping the baby in a white flannel blanket when Amy was seized by another contraction. All she had to do was point to the towels on the nightstand and he understood. They were a team now. He slid one towel in place beneath her, tucked the squalling bundle in the crook of his arm and massaged Amy's belly with the heel of his free hand. "You'll be all done in a New York minute, honey. Just one more good—"

"Awwwwfullll!"

"One more awful pain. God, I could never be a woman. You're amazing, Amy." In both will and body, he thought as she expelled the afterbirth. He rubbed hard. Her belly felt like rubber on the outside and rock underneath. "You made a miracle. I saw it with my own eyes."

The baby squawked angrily as Tate cradled her against his chest. "That's right, little darlin'. Take charge, just like your mama."

But it was Tate who was in charge. He folded the towel around the afterbirth and set it aside. Then he tucked another towel between Amy's legs and covered her with a sheet. She needed a moment to catch her breath.

"Tate?"

He turned, and Jody offered up several towels. "Thanks, partner. Look what we've got." Jody lifted his chin for a peek. Tate chuckled, knowing the crinkled red face hardly met the little boy's expectations.

He sat on the bed and leaned close to Amy. "Soon as I get this little gal acquainted with her mother's face, maybe she won't be quite so..."

The bawling subsided to a whimper when Amy took the baby in her arms. Weary as she was, her pale face lit up like a firefly in a jar.

"That's better," he said. "She wasn't expecting to see my fuzzy face first thing."

"She's glad you were there," Amy said, her eyes smiling up at him. "So am I."

"I never thought I'd..." He shook his head as all words failed him. They looked so pretty together, triumphant mother and tiny daughter. Tate knew damn well he was blushing head to toe. "I'd better clean things up a little."

"Things?"

"You and her." He wasn't sure what to do for Amy now. He knew she might need stitches. The sooner he put in a call for medical help, the better. Then he was going to dispose of the contents of the towel....

"We have to save that," Amy said, reading his intentions. Baffled, he figured the pain had taken its toll on her senses. "It goes in the freezer downstairs, and then into the ground next spring when I plant the baby's tree."

"Oh." He shrugged. "Whatever you say."

"Jody has a tree. Don't you, Jody?" Jody nodded, gratified to hear his name. "Come here and say hello to your new sister. I'm fine now, see? I'm just fine."

The back door opened, and a woman's voice called out, "Anybody home?"

"Mrs. Massey," Amy explained.

The bespectacled woman appeared in the bedroom doorway. Curiously, Tate heard no great flood of relief in Amy's greeting. "You just missed it, Mrs. Massey."

"I can see that." The stocky, middle-aged woman took account, acknowledging Tate with a nod as she removed her red quilted jacket. "My, my, my. Did you steal my job away?"

"I hope I didn't do anything... I mean, I hope I didn't make any mistakes."

"You didn't," Amy said happily. "You were wonderful. I don't know what I would have done if—"

"I should have been here earlier."

"I think that's my line," Mrs. Massey said. "But there are some little details I can attend to. I'm going to scrub up while you put that floor lamp right there next to the bed." She chucked Jody under the chin on her way back out the door. "What do you think, Jody? A brand-new baby. Isn't it fun?"

"Fun?" Hell of a way to spend Saturday night, Tate thought. Then he realized the sun had dawned somewhere along the line and it was actually Sunday morning. He shared a conspiratorial smile with Amy. "How are you feeling? Having fun yet? Can I bring you anything?"

"Mrs. Massey will tie up the loose ends, so to speak."

"I tied one up myself." He was grinning like a kid who'd hit a grand slam.

"Yes, you did. Thank you."

"You sure have a hell of a way of soberin' a guy up, lady." He couldn't understand how he could be steady as a rock and still feeling so high. "Both of you ladies. Look at her. She's sucking on her little hand."

Amy's hand went to the buttons on her nightgown. "Maybe I ought to—"

"Before you do that, let me do my little job," Mrs. Massey instructed as she swooped back into the room.

Tate leaned out of her way, but he was in no hurry to relinquish his post. He wasn't sure he liked the way the midwife took over on the baby, peeling the blanket back to scrutinize her.

"Oh, look at her color. Just what we like to see. Nothing old, nothing new, nothing borrowed, and especially nothing too blue."

Mrs. Massey gave the baby her first test and announced that her score was outstanding. Tate's suspicions fell away as he suppressed the urge to applaud. The woman recognized a perfect kid when she saw one. He was surprised when she bundled the baby back up in the flannel blanket and handed her to him.

"Now, if you and Jody would like to clean the little one up a bit while I tend to Amy..."

"She's so little." And she didn't want a bath. He could tell by the scrunched-up look in her face. "You mean just wash her with ordinary water?"

"Body temperature," Mrs. Massey instructed. "Water will comfort her. You can handle it. You've done fine so far."

He looked down at the tiny prunelike face nestled in the blanket, then glanced at Amy. She looked exhausted, but she nodded, her eyes bright with approval. Even now it amazed him to think she trusted him to take the precious bundle in his big, clumsy hands and leave the room. Instead of pleading incompetence he heard himself promise, "I'll be real careful."

"Jody knows where her clothes are," Amy said. "Jody, remember which drawer has the baby clothes?" Jody bobbed his head. "Will you pick out a little shirt like the one Tate's wearing and a little tiny sleeper like yours?"

"And a baby diaper?"

"Yes, and the pins."

"And get the baby bath stuff?" He was out the door, sliding down the hallway on slick pajama feet. "I know where the baby bath stuff is, Tate. We have a baby towel, too."

Tate followed him to the third bedroom, which had been decorated in white and soft pastels for the long-awaited occupant. Jody opened the third bureau drawer and took out a white sleeper with a row of pink lambs marching across the yoke. "This brand-new one," he decided and held it up for Tate's review.

"Your mother will definitely approve."

"And here's the shirt, and these baby pants to keep her clothes dry and a—"

"What do you think, Jody? I say we turn the heat up a little and treat her just like a newborn calf that maybe took a chill, huh?"

"Uh-huh."

"You're just lucky there was an experienced cow-hand in the house tonight, baby girl. And a little broomstick cowboy in training." He might have plopped a calf into the washtub downstairs, but he figured the kitchen sink would work better for this job. He closed the blind against the morning sunlight streaming through the window. Too much shock for a little person fresh out of the womb.

"We're a team, right, Jody?"

"Uh-huh." Jody climbed up on a chair and handed Tate a bottle of liquid baby soap and a soft hooded towel. "This is the stuff we have to use. She sure has messy hair."

"And a lot of it."

Mrs. Massey was right. The water seemed to soothe the infant. Tate ladled it over her with one hand as he cradled her head in his other palm. He didn't want to mess too much with her face, and he figured the white, waxy stuff was probably nature's cold cream, so he left it alone. But he knew a lady didn't like having sticky stuff in her hair. That had to go.

"Your next job is to find the hair dryer, partner."

"I know where it is!" And Jody was off like a shot.

"She's all cleaned up now," Tate announced as he lowered the fussy little one into her mother's arms. "She's just as pretty as a Thoroughbred filly, and she wants her mama right now."

"Oh, yes, come here, sweetie."

"Before I go, I have a few instructions for you menfolk," Mrs. Massey said. "Starting with taking care of Mom. After she rests, we want her to get up and walk a little, but we don't want her to overdo. It's up to you boys to do the cooking and the cleaning up for a few days, you got that? Because if you leave a mess in the kitchen, she's not going to rest until she gets it cleaned up."

"I'm not an invalid, Mrs. Massey."

"She's been using that line on me ever since I started to work for her," Tate said. "I'll snub her to the bed-post if I have to."

"You're the—" the older woman glanced at Amy, then back to Tate "—hired hand?" He affirmed the title with a humble shrug, and she laughed. "Well, now you can *really* claim to be a jack-of-all-trades. I'll be stopping by daily for a while, but you call me if you need anything." She turned to Amy. "You know what kind of bleeding to expect. Anything heavy, any diz-ziness or fainting—" The finger was pointed Amy's way, but the final charge was given to Tate. "—she goes to the hospital."

"Got it."

"Don't let that baby keep her from getting her rest. Got a name for her yet?"

"Karen," Amy said—reverently, because it was the first time. "Karen Marie Becker."

It was a nice name, Tate thought. He had an aunt named Karen, but she lived in Texas. And his moth-er's name had been Mary. He liked it. Karen Marie...Becker.

Of course it was Becker. She was Kenny's daugh-ter. He'd just helped to bring his best friend's daugh-ter into the world, given her her first bath and dressed her for the first time. And now she had a name.

Nothing wrong with Karen Marie Becker...except that when Amy had said that last part out loud, it had felt like a pinprick in his euphoric bubble.

Mrs. Massey gave him a colleague's pat on the back before she left, declaring that more duty called her. "The stork's having a field day in Overo. Now that you've got your feet wet, how about—"

"Not a chance," Tate demurred with palms raised in self-defense. "I don't care to press my luck."

"Luck, schmuck. The Lord doesn't always give us what we think we want, but most times He gives us what we need." She punctuated her homily with a nod and a smile. "He gave you stork wings last night, Mister Hired Hand."

Stork wings? Tate flexed the muscles in his back as he watched Mrs. Massey back her Blazer down the driveway. He did feel a pinch right above the shoulder blades.

He stuck his head in the door of Amy's bedroom. "Can I get you anything? A glass of milk maybe— whoa!" A short-armed tackle pinned him around the knees. He looked down, and Jody looked up, pleading to be noticed.

"Jody..." Amy applied the universal mother's warning tone.

"You got a steer wrestler's grip, there, partner." Tate lifted the boy into his arms. "We got our instructions, and we're at your service, ma'am."

"Karen might take you up on that glass of milk. It's slim pickings until mine comes in."

The baby was asleep in her mother's arms. Tate and Jody looked on like shepherds in a crèche.

"Is there colostrum?" Tate asked absently. He glanced up and caught her eyes laughing at him. Hell, he didn't know. He was just curious.

"Like with cows and sheep? Yes, for the first few days. We mammal mamas are all the same."

"So, you want some kind of oat—" he winked at Jody and teased Amy with a grin "—meal?"

"I want you to sit with us. You and Jody." She nodded toward the wicker rocker next to the bed.

"C'mon, cowboy," Tate said. "Come take a ride on your partner's knee."

"We couldn't have managed this without you two." Amy touched the baby's cheek. "She came a lot quicker than Jody did. She didn't give me much warning at all."

"Women are like that. You never know what to expect." Tate jiggled his knee, and Jody bobbled happily. "You remember that, partner. Every woman's got her own timing, and there's no point in a man tryin' to set his watch by it."

"I can't think of a single comeback, so I guess we'll let that one stand." She smiled at the sleeping infant. "For now. Right, Karen? When they're good, they're very, very good. And today they were incredible."

"And whenever you're willin' to give in that easy, you have to be very, very tired," Tate observed. "We've already put in a big day, and there's still about sixteen hours to go. You're one of those bosses that doesn't give a guy time to sleep it off."

"I think we'll all be napping today." She couldn't take her eyes off the tiny, tranquil face. "One of us has already started."

"And one more is on her way." Time for the boys to take their leave. "That's you, so if you've got any other surprises, lay them on me before I head out to the barn to get started on the chores. I've got another load of hay coming today."

"No more surprises. Just gratitude."

"Just doin' my job, ma'am."

"You need rest, too," she told him.

"I'll get it eventually." Tate grinned. "Now, if I was a sheepherder, I could lie around on the hillsides all day and do all kinds of cloud-dreamin', but a cowboy's work is never done."

But it didn't matter. Today he had adrenaline to spare.

He'd never imagined himself holding a baby, much less delivering one. Thinking about it made him feel a little weak in the knees. When he told Myron Olson about it, he couldn't help grinning like a sailor on shore leave. Myron was so tickled, he offered to throw in another load of hay. Tate told him he could bring over another horse, too.

He climbed into the driver's seat of Amy's big John Deere 4020. He was beginning to feel the effects of lack of sleep. Once he got Myron's flatbed unloaded and fed all his charges, he figured he would be ready to hit the hay himself.

He didn't know how the dogs had gotten out, but they were making fools of themselves again, chasing a damn tumbleweed. As he started backing the tractor he took a quick check over his shoulder. For a split second he saw Jody's face looking up at him just be-

yond the rolling ridges of one big black tire. Then it
was just the tire.

The whole sky toppled over on him. He heard a
piercing scream, and for a moment the world went
black. His legs wouldn't work, nor would his arms,
and his head wouldn't turn. He was surrounded by
shouting, and the scream rose in terror, pitched so high
it was beyond the reach of his ears. It was infinite,
soundless, nameless and timeless.

When the scream plummeted back to the present, it
was lodged in his own throat. He whirled and spat it
out as he dropped to the ground. And there stood
Jody, looking up at him, wide-eyed, trusting and in-
nocent as always.

Trembling terror overrode reality as Tate towered
over the child. He leaned down, his big hands laying
claim to slight shoulders, making sure they were real.
Sweet Lord, he hadn't been touched, had he? He was
still in one—

"I damn near ran over you, boy!"

"I f-found my horse's ear." Shyly, Jody displayed
a scrap of leather, as if such an offering might as-
suage the big man's anger.

"Jody, I just barely saw you. I almost..." Tate
sputtered, his heart racing. He pointed a gloved finger and commanded with all the fervor of Moses,
"You go in the house now. I'll look at that later. You
go inside and stay out of the way."

He saw Jody's lip quiver, saw the tears welling in the
little boy's eyes as he turned and ran toward the house.
The same tears burned deep in his own brain. Remembered tears. God, it could happen all over again,
so easily, in the blink of an eye. He turned and stared

the damn tractor down, its bucket-loader lifted skyward as if to say, "Don't blame me. It's Tate Harrison again."

Damn, he hated operating farm equipment. He would rather buck out a horse any day. At least then the only neck he was likely to break was his own.

The house was quiet when he went back inside. He thought about looking for Jody first thing, but he felt so bad about the way he'd barked at him that he decided to make supper instead. He wondered what a person who'd just had a baby would feel like eating. He wondered whether a little person who'd just had his butt chewed out by a big person with a thick head would feel like eating anything at all. Down at the end of the hallway, behind the closed bedroom door, he could hear the baby, bleating like a hungry lamb. The crying ceased abruptly, and Tate wondered whether little Karen was getting real milk yet.

Too soon, he thought, but obviously Amy was able to give the baby what she needed. He wished he had something like that to give Jody right now. Something warm and nourishing, something that would flow easily, without worthless apologies or asinine explanations. Hell, Jody was just a little boy. Tate was the one who had a history of being careless. *Tate* was the one.

He stood awkwardly outside Amy's door, flexed his hand a couple of times before he rapped his knuckles on the wood and quietly announced himself. "Are you girls decent? Can I bring in some food?"

"Come in." Amy braced herself and slid up gingerly, reaching around to adjust her pillows. "Oh, my, we've just been sleeping and nursing, nursing and sleeping. Karen's sleeping again."

"Figured you'd fed her." He handed her a mug of chicken soup, then stuffed an extra pillow behind her. "Figured *I'd* feed *you*."

"Thank you." She smiled sleepily. "Just for today. You won't have to do this tomorrow."

"I want to." He sat on the edge of the bed. "I'm not real great at it, but I can open a can."

"Have you and Jody eaten?"

"We will in a minute. I wasn't sure where...I mean, I thought he might be in here with you. Guess he must be in his room." He glanced at the bassinet he'd brought in earlier and set next to the bed, within Amy's reach. It hadn't been too long since Jody had slept in that little straw bed. "Did he tell you . . . that I acted like a jerk a while ago?"

"What do you mean?"

"I didn't know he was outside. I was backing up the tractor. He was standing pretty close." He closed his eyes and gave his head a quick shake. "I...I made him go in the house."

"There's nothing wrong with that, Tate."

"Yeah, but I yelled at him. I haven't been around kids much. All I know is when a calf tries to get himself into a bad place, you put a scare into him, send him packing." He couldn't look at her, but he could feel her looking at him. He could feel her waiting. "I scared Jody. I scared him worse than—" he swallowed hard "—worse than he scared me."

"You yelled at him? Is that all?" she asked quietly, and he heard the fear in her voice.

"I grabbed him by the shoulders. I was so glad he was still standing there, I don't know if I held him too tight, but I shouted right in his face and I...I told him to stay out of the way. Like I was tellin' him it was his fault, when it was mine." He turned to her, his voice as doleful as autumn rain. "I didn't hit him. I wouldn't do that, I swear."

"I didn't think you would, Tate." Wearily he rose to his feet. She caught his hand. "What are you going to do?"

"See if he's awake. Ask him if he's hungry." He squeezed her hand, then let it go as he stepped back from the bed.

"Tell him why you shouted at him."

"What difference does it make why?" Her eyes held his until he knew he needed the answer for himself. "I was scared stupid, that's why."

"Tell him that."

"What if he doesn't want me..." *Around him. Close to him. Breathing his air.* "...want to look at me or anything?"

"Give him the benefit of the doubt, Tate. He's a very mature four-year-old. He knows about safety and responsibility. I've taught him that." She nodded encouragingly. "Just ask him if he's hungry. That'll be a start."

He found Jody sprawled on his stomach, driving his toy cars down the parallel roads in the hardwood floor in his bedroom. He looked up, surprised, but he lowered his chin quickly and went back to his cars.

"Don't mean to interrupt, but I've got some supper ready."

"Not hungry."

"Your mom said you liked those little baby hot dogs in the can. I fixed you some with biscuits and soup." Jody looked up again. "And some chocolate milk," Tate added, encouraged. "You like chocolate milk?"

Jody rolled his toes against the wood and wagged his heels back and forth. But his belly seemed glued to the floor.

Tate noticed the broomstick horse lying on the bed, along with the detached leather ear. Moving like old molasses, he made himself walk over to the bed. He picked up the broken toy as he seated himself. He felt like a giant in a dollhouse sitting on the youth bed, which hadn't been made that day. The sheets were printed with teddy bear cowboys riding rocking horses and spinning perfect loops above their ten-gallon hats.

"I promised I'd fix this, didn't I?"

"I found the ear in my toy box," Jody reported as he lined two cars up side by side.

"And that was good finding." Tate watched him add a third car to the row, then a fourth. "I'm sorry I yelled at you before." A yellow car came into line, but this one drove up slowly. "I know I sounded like I was mad at you. I wasn't. Not really."

With his thumb on its roof Jody rocked the yellow car back and forth on its diminutive wheels. "I'm not supposed to get around the tractor when it's running," he confided quietly. "The tires are big, and the PTO can grab my hair or my shirt and really get me hurt."

"That's right." As formidable as the huge tires were, the tractor's power takeoff was an appalling threat, and the danger of lost limbs was one of the earliest warnings every ranch kid heard. "Your mom has told you all that, huh?"

"Oh, yeah. And my dad." He sat up, pivoted on his bottom and looked up at Tate. "I just forgot for a minute."

"I know. That can happen." Tate glanced at the yellow car as he laced his fingers together. "You know what happened to me when I looked down and saw you there?"

"No."

"I was scared I was gonna hit you. And I yelled at you because I was mad at myself for not seeing you sooner." His eyes darted back to the anxious little face. "The driver is responsible, Jody. Not you. When you're driving a vehicle, you have to make sure there's nothing behind you, nothing in front of you that you might hit...."

But Tate realized that there was only one thing the boy understood. The big man had been as threatening as the big tractor. "I'm sorry," Tate offered. "I didn't mean to yell at you. It wasn't your fault. It was mine." The boy hung his head. "I scared you, huh?"

Jody nodded. "I was a little bit scared."

"I was a lot scared." Tate lifted his hands and spread them in invitation, and Jody scrambled to his feet and came running. He threw his arms around Tate's neck with grateful abandon, and Tate closed his eyes and hugged him for all he was worth.

"It was a close call, Jody. You know what a close call is?"

"I could have got hit by the tractor?"

"After a close call is all over, it's too late to be scared, but it doesn't matter. It still haunts you for a while, kind of like a bad dream." He leaned back and looked Jody in the eye. "If I'd hurt you, I don't know what I would have done."

"You'd take me to the doctor, wouldn't you?"

"Yes, I would." He lifted the boy onto his lap. "I sure would. We're partners."

"We're partners."

"We birthed a baby together today, didn't we? You and me, we helped your little sister get born." Jody tested the prickliness of Tate's stubble against his palm, and Tate smiled. "'Course, your mom did most of the work. That's why she was making all that noise—because it's hard work pushing the baby out. That's why they call it *labor.* And now she needs rest, so we're gonna do all the work around here, 'cause she's done her share for a while."

"I can fix my own bed, and I can feed Daisy and Duke and Cinnamon Toast."

"And I can feed you," Tate said as he patted Jody's bottom. "You ready to eat?"

Not quite. Jody was still thinking. "It scared me more when *she* yelled," he mused. "I never heard her yell like that before."

"And then I yelled, and you must think all the grown-ups went crazy today. But we're okay now. It's been a crazy, terrible, fantastic day, and we made it through." He squeezed Jody's shoulder. "So let's have ourselves something to eat."

"Are you gonna shave?" Jody asked as they headed toward the kitchen.

"Prob'ly I should."

"Can I watch?"

Amy laid her head back against the pillow and closed her eyes. Tate Harrison was such a difficult man to figure out. One minute he was out boozing with Overo's hell-raisers, and the next he was bringing her daughter into the world with more levelheadedness and every bit as much tender concern as she might have expected from her child's own father. She'd never seen Tate more shaken than he'd been today, or more jubilant.

Vigilant as any brooding hen, she was glad she'd been able to eavesdrop on the conversation he'd had with Jody across the hall. She wasn't sure what to make of the terrible guilt she'd seen in Tate's eyes when he'd told her about the incident with Jody, but she knew he had not harmed her son. She breathed a long, gratified sigh. She was fundamentally independent, but she had trusted Tate with a most intimate and momentous task, and he had come through for her in spades. Thank God she could continue to trust him with her son.

She wasn't going to start relying on him, she reminded herself. The man's feet were made of sand. But he had more heart than she'd ever given him credit for, and she was hoping she could lean on that particular muscle and a few others until she could truly get back on her feet again. She wouldn't *depend* on his support. But as long as he was willing to stay, it wouldn't hurt to lean on it, just a little.

Chapter Six

When Amy's milk came in her breasts blew up like twin beach balls. Tate had never seen anything like it. He'd brought her a sandwich and discovered, once again, a changed woman. He tried not to stare, but she caught him at it. She laughed, he thought quite charitably. He stared at the toes of his boots, then tried to zoom back up to her face. But his damned eyes were drawn right back to the same amazing transformation in her otherwise almost-back-to-normal body.

He shook his head and gave up trying to be cool. "Are they gonna stay like that?"

Now she howled. "Lord have mercy, I have finally arrived. Voluptuous at last."

"Well, either way, I mean . . . I always thought you had a nice—" *Chest on you.* He tore his eyes away as he groped for an alternative. "*Shape*. Really nice. But, you know, this is ... nice, too."

"They won't stay this way long." She accepted the proffered plate and gave a quick shrug. "My milk just came in with a vengeance is all."

"Do they hurt?"

"Suck in a real deep breath." He complied. "Now suck in some more. Now a little more. Feel like you're gonna bust yet?" He nodded. She took up the sandwich. "Now hold it for a couple of days and see if it hurts."

He deflated quickly. "I gotta give up those cigarettes. Damn, that pinches."

"Exactly." Amy set her own lunch aside on the signal of soft baby murmurs. "Would you like to hand me my little milk drainer?"

Tate stepped over to the bassinet. Karen had kicked off her pink blanket, tiny legs churning involuntarily. He folded it around her and lifted her in his hands. She was cranking up to cry, but she changed her mind when he cuddled her against his chest. He liked the sweet little sounds she made, even though she was rooting around a dry well.

"Can't help you there, little girl. Your mama's got what you want and then some." He shifted Karen for the transfer as he came to the side of the bed. "You got a preference which side?"

"Ready on the right, ready on the left."

The buttons on Amy's nightgown already lay open between her bulging breasts. Tate swallowed hard. Amy pulled her white gown aside as he laid the baby in the crook of her left arm, positioning the little pink cheek near the source of mother's milk. The miniature mouth fit over the distended nipple like a trailer coupling. Tate felt a surge of excitement that had nothing to do with hunger and little to do with sex. Pride, maybe. He wasn't ogling, but he was having a hell of a time tearing his eyes away.

"Would you hand me a bath towel off the dresser?" Amy asked.

He snatched it up and returned to her, glanced in her eyes for permission, then admired the tranquil activity at her breast again. A wet spot was quickly growing over her right breast, and he understood the need for the towel. Impulsively he knelt beside the bed. She lifted her right elbow. He tucked the towel under her side and arranged it over her breast.

"I keep getting everything wet."

"I'll change the bed when you're done." The baby's contented little noises made him smile. "Seems like a waste of good produce."

"There's such an abundance to start with. If I were a ewe, I'd probably have twins. Two mouths to suckle."

Now it *did* have something to do with sex, something to do with a man's urge to kiss a woman at the damnedest times. His head was falling fast. He was drowning in her eyes, sinking like a stone, going under for the third time. When the authorities dredged up his corpse, it would be obvious where he carried the lead weight that had pulled him under. He hoped she would be able to explain it away in the eulogy.

Amy saw it coming, and she met it head-on with a warm, wet, open-mouthed kiss.

Just one kiss, but it was a real breath-stealer. When it was over, he couldn't quite draw away. Forehead to forehead they rested, their mouths sharing hot breath, their nostrils filled with the scent of sweet milk.

"I couldn't help myself," he whispered.

"It's all right." She drew a long, slow breath. "A woman needs a man's kiss when she's..." He lifted his head and looked expectantly into her eyes. She glanced away. "I heard you talking to Jody. I get scared, too, sometimes. When I realized I was in labor, and I knew I was alone, I really got scared."

She wasn't alone now. He wanted her to know that. He cupped his hand around her cheek and kissed her again, more gently this time. He couldn't remember when he'd ever gotten down on his knees to kiss a woman. He told himself that he just wanted to assure her that he was there, but her lips were remarkably responsive, and she tasted so damn good.

She took his hand, put it on her belly, then covered it with hers and pressed it tight. He felt a bulge in her stomach, but it was hard, like muscle.

"It hurts when the baby nurses," she explained quietly. "It's nature's way of making my uterus contract back down to size, but it..." Her fingers dug into the back of his hand. He took the hint and began kneading the knot in her belly. "I've had enough of pain," she said.

"Yes, you have." If he could take it away, he would thank her for the privilege. "It doesn't seem fair. It was hard to watch you suffer with it. It's no wonder you were scared."

"I was afraid for my baby. I was afraid I wasn't strong enough." She tipped her head back against the pillow, eyes closed as she remembered. "I was going to call someone else, the sheriff or someone, but I was afraid it was too late for anyone to..." She gave him her soft earth-mother smile. "Thank you for coming back in time, Tate."

"I shouldn't have left."

He never should have left Overo in the first place, not without her. He should have stayed and fought for her instead of letting Kenny...

Oh, hell, he'd been through all this before, beating himself up inside in a way that no other judge or critic could manage. It was pointless. Kenny was the family man, not Tate.

"I shouldn't have left at all *that night,*" he clarified, still kneading her gently. "I knew your time was close. I shouldn't have left you alone."

"But you're not my husband, so you didn't owe me that kind of commitment."

"No." He knew she meant to absolve him. He wasn't sure why it felt like a rejection. "I'm not your husband. But I'm your husband's best friend. I'm, uh..." Reluctantly he drew his hand back and pushed himself to his feet. "Committed to him. His memory. To taking good care of his wife and his—"

"Tate, don't—"

"And his kids. Anything for Kenny's family. You need anything—food, sheets, towels..." He tossed her a cocky wink. "You need a man's kiss, honey, you just call on me anytime."

* * *

He brooded on that scene for the rest of the day. He would have gone into town and gotten himself good and drunk if it weren't for the fact that there was so damn much work to do around the place. That night he fixed Jody's broomstick horse. He gave it a new horsehair mane. He'd culled the black hair from a trimming he'd given the gelding he'd stopped thinking of as Kenny's horse and started calling Outlaw. He fixed the ears and the frayed rein, and he gave it a whole new broomstick.

Jody's response to the refurbished toy couldn't have been more rewarding for Tate if he'd bought the boy something grand and new and presented it all tied up with a big red bow. Jody announced that his horse's new name was Outlaw, Jr., and that he was going to ride him "up and down and all around the town." He was Amy's mounted escort when she went out to the barn "just to say hello" to a ewe that Tate had brought back from the pasture and treated for foot rot. And Tate was the baby-sitter.

"How's my little girl?" he whispered as he knelt beside the bassinet. Since nobody but Karen could hear him, he figured he could indulge himself in the possessive claim. The baby knew what he meant. She grabbed his forefinger, and they shook on it.

He liked the soft little baby sounds she made as she waved her fist and turned her head from side to side, trying to focus on his face. "What are you telling me, huh? What do you see? It's not your mama's face. Kinda bristly. Needs a shave, same as it did the first time you saw it. Remember how you bawled? Was I that scary?"

He picked her up, taking a yellow flannel blanket with her, and he held her high against his shoulder. "Not anymore, huh? Wanna go for a little walk and see some more stuff?" *Just you and me, kid. Nobody else hears me babbling like this.* "You know what? You're not scary anymore, either. I've gotten used to you being such a little tyke."

He rubbed her flannel-covered back as he carried her into the living room, just for a change of scene. "'Course, this is as little as you'll ever be. Next time I come to visit..." She rewarded his back rubbing with what seemed like a very big burp for one so small. Having unwittingly done her a service, he smiled as he went on talking. "Well, you'll be a lot bigger next time. You'll be walking tall and talking big, just like your brother, Jody." His smile faded as he stared out the window at the distant mountain peaks. "And you won't remember me."

Amy came through the back door with a mighty, "Whew! Feels like I just ran the marathon." Tate could hear "Outlaw, Jr." clopping at her side across the kitchen floor. Amy looked surprised when she saw him in the living room with the baby. "Is she already hungry again?"

"No, but she was awake, and she's wantin' to tell the world hello, too, just like her mama."

"I have to get active and get my strength back." Her cheeks were rosy. From where Tate stood she was looking pretty bright-eyed, bushy-tailed and back in charge as she took the baby from him. "I'll make supper," she said.

"Tired of my canned soup and cold meat sandwiches?"

"I know you guys are ready for a change. Chicken and dumplings?" A pint-size lasso loop landed over the back of a chair. "Jody, I asked you not to do that in the house. Maybe Tate could give you a bike-riding lesson while I make supper?"

"We could play with the baby while you cook," Tate suggested.

"She doesn't know how to play." She rocked the baby in the crook of her arm. "And anyway, she's almost asleep."

"C'mon, partner." Disgusted, Tate reached for his jacket. "We're gettin' kicked out of the kitchen."

"It'll be worth your while, I promise."

Yeah, right. Tate left the house feeling as peevish as a wet cat. Jody followed at his heels in the same mood. He kicked a tire on his bicycle as he passed it in the yard. Tate turned, one eyebrow cocked solicitously.

"I don't wanna ride that ol' bike." Jody pouted. "I like to ride horses. When I get big, I'm gonna have a real horse, but I won't fall off, and I won't get killed. I'm gonna be a cowboy, like you."

"What should we do with this?" Tate's nod indicated the bike.

"Put it in the shed."

"Good idea." He lifted the offending toy by its handlebars, and they headed for the shed together. "Out of your mother's sight, out of her mind, huh?"

"She just came out here and petted that ewe that's limping around, and then she went back to that baby."

"Uh-oh." Tate remembered what it was like to be upstaged by an attention-grabbing new baby. "How do you like the new baby, Jody?"

"She doesn't *do* nuthin'. She just cries and smells funny." Jody kicked at the gravel in his path. "I told you a brother would be better than a sister. I wanted a baby brother."

"And I told you, they're both the same at first. They don't do much. Karen couldn't go out to the corral with me and help me feed Outlaw."

"I could!"

"And since she can't even sit up yet, I couldn't put her up on Outlaw's back and lead her around."

"You could do that with me. I can sit up." His feet suddenly stopped dragging.

By the time they'd reached the shed, Tate wondered whether Jody had springs on the bottoms of his tennis shoes. "That's just what I was thinkin'. The thing is, we might not wanna mention it to your mom." He spared the boy a warning glance as he turned the handle on the door. "I mean, unless she asks. Then we'd have to 'fess up."

"What does *'fess up* mean?"

"Means a cowboy tells the truth when his mom puts a question to him. It's part of the code."

"What's a code?"

He didn't mind Jody's questions. He took a shot at answering every one. Too many of his own questions had been ignored when he was a kid, and he'd been looking for answers ever since. He'd found a few, but he was still looking for the big ones. Fortunately, either Jody hadn't thought up the big questions, or he'd decided to break Tate in easy. Baby girls were easily explained. Women were something else.

At bedtime Amy read Jody two extra stories, sticking with it until he fell asleep. When she returned to her room, she was surprised to find Tate sitting on the bed with Karen. Wonder of wonders, he was pinning on a clean diaper. Amy tried to remember the last time she'd seen a man voluntarily tend to that particular chore.

"I was eavesdropping on the stories again," he admitted. "Jody says he wants to be a cowboy, and when he follows me out to the pickup, he tries to take steps as big as mine." Intent on his job, he didn't look up until he'd finished carefully fastening the second pin. "But he's not quite done being your first baby."

"I'm afraid he's going to grow up faster than either of us really wants him to."

"Either of *us?*"

"Either him or me." She couldn't help smiling. "I never thought I'd see Tate Harrison change a baby's diaper."

"Nothin' to it. Right, Karen?" He slid both hands under the baby and lifted her to his shoulder. "Only one thing ol' Tate can't do for you, and that's feed you. That's up to Mom, whose—" his eyes danced mischievously as he glanced at Amy "—jugs appear to be getting smaller, so I'd say you'd better get while the gettin's still good."

"Jugs?" She postured, hands on hips. "You'd better watch it, cowboy."

"Hey, just because you domesticate me a little, it doesn't mean I'm show-ring material."

She glanced down at her chest. "There's no less milk, just a little less pouf. I'm not show-ring material, either."

"You did a lot today." He piled the pillows against the headboard to make a backrest for her as she joined him on the bed. "I read somewhere that having a baby's like having major surgery. Takes a while to get your strength back."

"Where did you read that?"

"One of the magazines in that pile downstairs." Reluctantly Tate handed the baby over to her mother.

"Wouldn't be Ken's old *Quarter Horse Journal*s. Must be one of my old *Parents* magazines."

"Yeah, well, I've already read all the horse stuff." He planted his hands on his knees. "I'll go check on—"

"Stay, Tate." She worked the buttons on her nightgown with one hand. "We haven't talked much since—" the soft look in her eyes personalized her invitation "—since the last time you watched me do this."

"You don't mind if I watch you take your—" That's not it, he told himself, and he gripped his knees a little tighter as the last button slid though its hole. "Watch you feed the baby?"

"You've seen all there is to see. More than my husband saw, in fact." The blue-flowered flannel slid away, baring her round, scarlet nipple. "I went to the hospital when I had Jody. Kenny wasn't there."

"Really?" Tate didn't want to know why. He didn't want to talk about Kenny at all right now. Not with Amy's breast bared for the baby and blessings bestowed on his voyeurism. He wondered whether her nipples were sore. "Do you need a towel?"

"I have one." She patted the bed, offering him the spot right next to her. "I promise not to squirt you."

"You could squirt me?" Mesmerized, he moved closer.

"On a good day I have a six-foot range."

"Does it taste like regular milk?" He glanced up and caught her smiling indulgently, the way he might look at Jody. Hell, he had his questions, too. He told himself to watch the baby suckle, think warm milk, and he would have the general idea. "I guess I've had it, but I don't..."

She uncovered her free breast.

He lifted his gaze to hers. "...remember."

She couldn't make the offer in words, but her eyes were willing, mainly because he'd always been so easy on them. He was a beautiful man. His dark eyes held her gaze as he dipped his head slightly. Then he glanced down at the blue-white liquid dribbling down the underside of her breast. His full, sensuous lips parted as he looked into her eyes one more time to make sure. She nodded almost imperceptibly. He touched her nipple with the tip of his tongue.

She held her breath as he passed his tongue back and forth. The flow increased, and he took the bud of her nipple gently between his lips and let the milk leak into his mouth. He was cautious, like a humble petitioner, asking only to glean the overflow, while the tiny mouth on the left side was all business, working her like a milkmaid.

"Is it awful?" Amy asked timidly.

He made a low, contented sound, brushing his nose against her, scarcely moving his head in demurral. She forgot about her soreness. She forgot about feeling a little shy around him because she had been extraordinarily vulnerable and exposed, and she'd had time to reflect on what he might have seen and thought and felt. But for the moment misgivings and discomfort took a back seat in the presence of pure and natural tenderness.

He put his hand over her belly and felt for the distended muscle he'd learned so much about in recent days. He found it and massaged slowly, testing her receptiveness. "Does it still hurt here?" His lips hovered close to their post.

"Not as much, but..." *Yes, do that. Oh, yes, Tate, help me heal.*

"Will it hurt if I... suck a little?"

"Not if you're gentle."

He was gentle. The man who was wildness personified now suckled her with exquisite gentleness. She could not think how wanton she must be to permit such a thing. She could only feel. Deeply touched by the potential of his power bridled by his own tight control, she relinquished her doubts and permitted herself a separation from anxiety, however brief.

"It's warm and sweet," he murmured appreciatively. "Am I taking candy from the..." A tear slipped silently from the corner of Amy's eye and slid down her cheek. His heart fell with it.

"She's fallen asleep," Amy said quickly. He drew back, and she covered herself with her open nightgown as she got up to put Karen to bed. "Does it taste like candy?"

Propped on one elbow, feeling foolish and deserted, he watched her bend over the bassinet, absently clutching her nightgown together in front. What kind of stupid, juvenile thing had he done, and what in hell was he going to do with the ache it had left him with?

She straightened slowly and laid her hand over her eyes. His problem was minor. She turned, her face full of desolate tears and confusion, and he knew that, no matter who she was looking for on her bed, Tate Harrison was all she had. She sat down next to him. His problem was major again.

"Would you hold me for a while?" she asked.

"Sure." He reached for her, and she buried her face against his neck. He knew better than to expect an outpouring of emotion. This was Amy. She was stingy with her tears, and she sure as hell didn't shed them over spilled milk. "You were thinking about... somebody besides me."

"No." She put her arms around his middle and sighed. "Ken would never have done what you just did."

"I was just curious," he claimed.

She looked up at him, smiling through unshed tears.

"Okay, so maybe *curious* isn't the right word. Maybe I was just flyin' by the seat of my pants." Maybe that was exactly what he'd been doing since he'd first heard about Kenny's death, telling himself he had nothing but good intentions. "I'm sorry if I embarrassed you or made you feel . . . guilty or something."

She closed her eyes and buried her face again. This time he could feel her trembling. "Don't cry, honey."

"I can't help it," she sobbed. "I have to cry. Isn't that stupid?"

"No stupider than what I did. I didn't mean to do anything bad, I just—"

"It wasn't bad," she insisted, sniffling. "You were trying to make me feel . . . to help me . . ." She hated it when she got like this. "There's no reason for this ridiculous crying, so I'm stopping right now. See?" She used her hand until he plucked a tissue from the box on the night table and handed it to her.

She glanced ruefully at his shirt as she wiped her nose. "I'm getting you wet."

"Don't worry about it. It's a release, like we all need from time to time." *If she only knew.* "It's a natural thing, honey. Perfectly natural."

"Yes, I suppose. I try to convince myself I'm above those things, but obviously . . ." She gestured in frustration, the pink tissue balled up in her hand. "I do know the only thing I have to be embarrassed about is the way I've always—" She glanced up, red-eyed and apologetic. "I've always sold you short."

"You mean I ain't as cheap as what you thought?" he drawled with half a smile.

"It didn't surprise me that you bid the horses up. It was the kind of grand gesture I would have expected, and, after all, it was *only* money." Still shaky, she took a deep, steadying breath. "But the Tate Harrison I *thought* I knew would have walked away after that, satisfied he'd done his duty to his old *compadre.*"

He had come close to doing just that. "Honey, if I'd known you'd taken up sheepherdin'..."

"One favor," she entreated. "Try to remember not to call me 'honey.'"

"Is that what Kenny called you?"

"No." She smiled. "He called me 'Aims.' I don't want you to call me that, either." With a quick motion she erased the very idea. "I've heard you call at least a dozen other women 'honey.' It rolls off your tongue too easily, and it doesn't fit me."

"How about Bossy?"

She pressed her hand to her lactating breast and groaned.

"How about 'Black-Eyed Susan'?" he offered quietly, and the bittersweet reminder of "the road not taken" gave them both sober pause. He glanced away. "I'll come up with something better. Just give me a little time."

Her real question was, how much time would he give her?

His real question was, how much would she accept?

"Would you like me to fill the tub for you?" he asked.

"I guess you've noticed it's one of my favorite places to be lately."

"I can't imagine why." His smile faded as he searched her eyes. "Does everything...seem to be healing up the way it's supposed to? I asked Mrs.

Massey if everything was okay when she checked you over the other day, and she said, 'Just fine, and how are you?' Like I was askin' after *her* health.'' He gave a quick shrug. "Which I could have been, for all the conversation I had with her. She probably thought that was all the hired hand needed to know.''

"She's a woman of few words, and that was all the news. But I have one more important thing to say.'' She took his hand in hers, and he lost himself in her eyes. "Thanks for asking.''

He nodded. "Nice and warm, but not too hot, right?''

She nodded, too.

Half an hour later Amy emerged from the bathroom in her long white terry-cloth robe. Tate was watching TV in the living room when she came in to say good-night.

"Can I get you anything else?'' he offered as he rose from the chair. He'd made himself some coffee. "Maybe some milk or some tea?''

"If you don't stop being so nice, I'm going to start crying again.''

But she offered no objections when he took her in his arms again. Her hair was damp, and she smelled of strawberry soap. Hugging her felt right. Kissing her would feel even better. "Ask me to hold you through the night, Amy.''

"Tate, I can't have—''

"I know that. It's just good to hold you. It made me feel good when you asked me to.''

"I think maybe we're both kind of turned inside out right now, Tate. I know I am, and I know it would be

a mistake for us to spend the night in the same bed."
She leaned back and gripped his arms as she looked up
at him. "A big, big mistake."

"Turned inside out" was a good way of putting it.
He told himself to keep that in mind while he
straightened up the kitchen and thumbed through a
magazine. His damn ear had turned itself inside out.
He wasn't sure when he'd started keeping it cocked for
the baby's cry or for the sound of little pajama-
covered feet shuffling down the hallway.

He heard the telltale squeak of Jody's bedroom
door open. No footsteps. Amy was looking in on him.
Maybe she was thinking about changing her mind
about Tate. Maybe if Jody was sound asleep, and
maybe if Amy was having second thoughts about her
own empty bed, then *maybe* Tate wouldn't be spending another night tossing and turning on that wretched
cot.

But the family slept upstairs. Their hired hand slept
in the basement. Damn it all, it wasn't *his* family. She
wasn't his wife and they weren't his kids. He was doing it all for the *late* Kenny Becker, his best friend. He
heard her footsteps and the softer chirp Tate had
learned to recognize as the hinges on her bedroom
door. There was a pause.

"Good night, Tate."

"Good night."

By Thanksgiving there was snow, and it was time to
bring the sheep closer to home. Tate wanted to leave
Daisy and Duke at home, but Amy insisted that the
dogs would save him time. They might have saved

Amy time, but they were playing games with Tate this time out. When he dismounted and opened a gate, the dogs turned the herd and ran them down the fence line. Tate waved his arms and whistled and cussed to no avail. The sheep were scattered to hell and back, and all the dogs wanted to do was frolic in the wet snow.

By the time Tate had bunched the herd up again, the dogs were nowhere in sight, which was just fine by him. It was nightfall, and he was cold and hungry. He and Outlaw could push the herd without the help of any fancy dogs, just as soon as he figured out where the hell he was. The snow had thawed some during the day, but dropping temperatures had formed a crust that glistened by moonlight. The rolling hills all looked the same. But for the crunch of hooves breaking the snow crust and the creak of leather, the night was calm and quiet. It was the kind of night that used to bring Kenny over to his place for a moonlight ride.

This was no time to let himself start thinking about Kenny. Tate's butt was getting numb. His face was stiff with the cold. If Amy was his friend, she would have a hot bath and a shot of whiskey waiting for him.

But Kenny was his friend, or had been, and Tate had an eerie feeling that he was surveying the same moonscape Kenny had been looking at that last night. He sensed that he was hearing the last sounds Kenny had heard. "Did you lose your bearings that night, buddy?" he asked the night breeze. "Did you get turned around the way we used to sometimes?"

Kenny had been out joyriding that night. Tate was doing a job. He was trying to bring Amy's herd in.

Not that he was drawing any comparisons or thinking any critical thoughts concerning the dead.

"I never interfered with you, man, except that once. But she was your woman, 'til death do you part. And she misses you. Hell, *I* miss you. So I'm tryin' to do the right thing, here, helpin' her out." He tipped his hat in unconscious deference to the myriad stars. "She's one hell of a woman. She always was, even though it seemed like she was afraid to loosen up and just have fun."

Okay, so maybe his wits had left camp temporarily, but he figured he could count on the witnesses to keep his secret.

"I have a feeling you can hear me tonight, Kenny. Either that, or I'm talkin' to myself. Or a bunch of dumb sheep."

Amazing how close the big ewe's bleating resembled laughter.

"What's that, you big pile of wool? You're sayin' I'm the one who's lost? Hell, I know where I am. I'm back in Montana. Big Sky Country." He lifted his eyes to the diamond-studded, black velvet sky. "I hope. It damn sure ain't heaven if Tate Harrison's allowed in, right, buddy?"

Tate read his answer in the distant glow of Amy's yard light. He managed a stiff-lipped grin. "But it's likely as close as I'll ever come."

Chapter Seven

"Mom, where's Tate?"

Amy turned from the window. "He's bringing the sheep in, Jody." But the pens were still empty, the west gate was still closed and there was nothing stirring on the snow-covered hill above it. "He's out in the pasture, rounding up the sheep."

Jody was satisfied with Amy's answer for all of ten minutes, which was the time it took her to cut up vegetables for the stew she was planning for supper.

"Mom, when's Tate coming back?"

"Soon, Jody. He'll be back soon now." She glanced out the window again, this time noting the rosy streaks in the western sky. Sundown had a way of sneaking up on a person this time of year.

Not five minutes later Jody's broomstick horse was dragging its tail on the kitchen floor again. "Mom, what's taking Tate so—"

"I don't know!"

The moment the words were out, Amy regretted her tone. Jody's big eyes displayed the same kind of worry she'd been trying so hard to disown. He came to her and put his little arms around her hips, not looking for a hug, but offering one. She dropped to his eye level and took him in her arms.

"Tate rides really good," Jody assured her. "He hardly ever gets bucked off when he rides saddle bronc."

"Did he tell you that?"

"He showed me one of his buckles. They're like prizes you get for winning in rodeos. Tate rides *real* good."

So did your father. Horses were his life.

"You don't have to worry, Mom."

"You don't, either." She raked her fingers through the polka-dot horse's new mane. "Daisy and Duke aren't used to Tate, so he probably can't get them to work for him as fast as they do for me." The explanation sounded good. It even made sense.

It even made Amy herself actually smile. "Tate may be good with horses, but your mom is the dog expert around here." She gave Jody another good squeeze. "Of course, if he had the common sense of a good sheepherder, he'd take them the long way, which would take him safely along the highway. We could drive out a little ways and take a look."

Taking a look was better than sitting around worrying, Amy decided. She bundled up the children and drove her pickup several miles down the two-lane road, but there was no sign of sheep, dogs or horseman. Still nothing to worry about, she told Jody. If Tate was trying to get back before dark, he had to cut across the pasture. In that case, they wouldn't have been able to see him from the highway. But it was getting dark. When the dogs came back on their own, Amy called the sheriff.

"Miz Becker, it ain't all that cold out yet, and it ain't all that late," Sheriff Jim Katz told her over the phone.

Amy snorted disgustedly. When it got to be thirty below in the dead of winter, she would have to remember to ask the sheriff if it was cold enough for him yet.

"Man's got a job to do, y'gotta give him time to do it, Miz Becker."

"How long is that, Sheriff?" One glance at Jody's anxious face reminded her to curb the bitterness that burned the tip of her tongue. For the moment, anyway.

"I'd say ol' Tate oughta have them sheep penned up by eight and be warmin' up his innards at the Jackalope not long after. Once you start callin' the bars, if you can't track him down by midnight, you give me another call."

"Midnight. I'll make a note of that, Sheriff. Thank you."

"I understand you bein' touchy, Miz Becker. You've had more'n your share. But you gotta understand, I can't send out a search party every time a man rides out in his pasture.''

''It's mostly my pasture, and it's dark and Tate's not familiar with—''

''Tate Harrison knows his way around, Miz Becker.'' Katz chuckled. ''Give him a little more time. Then give a holler over to the Jackalope.''

Amy wasn't tracking *anybody* down at the Jackalope. Men never took anything seriously until the situation was long past serious. She went about her business, and feeding her children came first. Twice during supper she jumped up from the table to check on the noise she thought she'd heard outside.

After she cleaned up the dishes she congratulated herself for getting the laundry done during the off-peak hours when electricity rates were cheaper. She left the baskets of folded clothes downstairs, thinking she would ask Tate to carry them up. Not that she couldn't lift them herself, she mused as she glanced out the window for the fifteenth time, but knowing Tate, she would be in for a reprimand if he caught her at it. He would tell her it was too soon for her to be hauling heavy loads up the stairs.

She was the perfect image of calm, repeatedly reassuring Jody as she bathed both children. After she'd put them to bed, she showered and dressed for bed herself, even though she fully intended to keep vigil. She turned the lights out so she could see through the window, but nothing stirred in the bright circle cast by the yard light. Nothing—absolutely nothing. She folded her arms on the back of the sofa, rested her head in the nest they made and kept watch out the side window.

The yard light was a homing beacon, but Tate was disappointed to see that the house was dark. Not even a light left on in the kitchen. The vehicles were all lined up in a row, present and accounted for. No one was looking for him. That was a relief, of course. It didn't make any sense to take the kids out on a cold night and drive around looking when she wouldn't have had a prayer of finding him, anyway. Not on the trail he'd taken. He had half a mind to backtrack tomorrow and see just where in hell he'd been.

He got the sheep bedded down and his horse rubbed down. Outlaw deserved that and then some for getting him home—getting him *back,* back to the house. When he'd first seen that yard light, he'd really felt as though he'd found his way home. He'd had to remind himself that it was the Becker place. Just a house. Just a dark house, where everybody was tucked up in bed, nice and cozy the way they ought to be.

Amy sat bolt upright when the back door opened. Somehow she had let herself doze off, lost track of time, neglected her fretting. She sprang to her feet, but she managed to affect some measure of composure by the time she reached the kitchen.

"Tate?"

There he stood in the shadows just inside the door. He was safe. He was home at last. He was unscathed, breathing normally, filling her kitchen doorway with his broad shoulders and the fresh scent of a winter's night.

He glanced up from pulling his gloves off. "You still up?"

"I've been waiting, but I guess I dozed off." She crossed the cold floor on bare feet, stopping short of arm's reach. "Did you have trouble?"

"Damn dogs wouldn't listen to me," he complained. She could tell his lips were stiff. "Other than that . . . I kinda got lost. Whole countryside's crusted over with snow. Looks like a huge white lake. You try to set your course, and just when you think you've got yourself lined out, you cross your own tracks. Pretty soon you start talkin' to yourself, tryin' to keep your brain from wanderin' away from camp."

Now that he was inside, his teeth had started chattering. "I brought 'em all back, though." He fumbled with the buttons on his sheepskin coat. "Every last bleatin' one of 'em. I counted."

"Let me help you." Her heart pounded out a jubilant rhythm as she took over the job of undoing his buttons. "Are your fingers . . . ?"

"A little stiff, is all."

She pushed his jacket off his shoulders, then reached up to take his hat, then the scarf he'd tied under it. "How about your ears?"

He groaned when she put her hands over them. She knew the shock of her warmth must hurt, but he stood still for her inspection. There was even an indulgent smile in his voice. "They're still there."

"Oh, but so cold, and your cheeks . . ." Vulnerable places, all. She cupped her palms over his cheeks. If she turned on the light, would she find a healthy flame in his skin, or dark discoloration? She could feel his body shaking. Hers joined in, whether from relief or panic, she didn't know.

He put his hands over hers, sandwiching her warmth and pressing it to his face. She ached sympathetically with the stiffness in his hands.

"I don't know if I can get my boots off without a crowbar. My feet have turned to ice."

"I'll take them off. Sit here." She dragged a chair back from the table. The offer seemed to surprise him, but he complied, raising one leg so she could get a grip on his boot heel. "Can you wiggle your foot just a little?"

"Sorry, ma'am. 'Fraid I'm plumb out of wiggle."

"Okay, then, just hold still while I—" She turned her back, straddled his leg and tugged. His foot was forced to bend as the boot came loose, and he sucked his breath quickly between his teeth with the pain.

"If it hurts, you're starting to thaw," she said as she stepped over one leg and on to the next.

"I'm thawing, then. Hungry, too. Anything left from supper?"

"I'm going to fix you something, and it's also my turn to fill the tub for you, and I want to make sure..."

When the second boot came off, she found herself sitting on his knee. He settled his hands over her hips, and she looked at him over her shoulder. It was her turn to be surprised.

He grinned. "Why are we sittin' in the dark?"

Smiling shyly, she felt like a child sitting on Santa's knee. Partly uneasy, but mostly delighted. "Because I was watching out the window."

"I thought you'd gone to bed." He toyed with the white sash of her robe, tugging, turning her toward him. "The house was dark, so I thought..."

"I didn't know what to do. I took the kids and drove up the road. I called the sheriff, but he said to give you...to wait a while, to..." She closed her eyes as he touched her cheek. "Oh, Tate, your hands are still so cold."

"Your face is warm."

"I wasn't sure—"

His arms encircled her, and his kiss put an end to uncertainty. He was there, in the flesh. She touched his face, his ears, his neck, hoping to transfer her warmth to his chilled skin. But his lips were warm. His embrace tightened as he tilted his head for a new angle, for better access to her lips and the recesses of her mouth. She welcomed his tongue's gentle onslaught. She was more than glad to have him home.

She tucked her hands into the open neck of his flannel work shirt and smoothed them over cool combed cotton. He had the neck and shoulder muscles of a breeding stud. The feel of him thrilled her, and when he broke the kiss, she knew he could read that weakness in her eyes. He could hear it in every fluttery breath she took.

She traced his collarbones with her thumbs. "Just a plain T-shirt instead of long johns, Tate? What were you thinking?"

"It started out to be a nice...." He closed his eyes, and his mighty shoulders quivered beneath her hands. "Oh, God, Amy, if you wanna undress me all the way... my fingers are still pretty stiff."

It would hardly be a difficult task, she thought. She could easily warm his body with hers. She could readily banish the chill from his bones and ease whatever stiffness plagued him. It was so good to have him safe in her arms that it was hard to remember any doubts she'd ever had about holding him close.

About trying to hold him at all.

"Let me start the water." She got up quickly and pulled him out of the chair. "We need to get you into some warm water right away."

"I think I'm gonna like this part."

"It's all part of thawing out. How do you like it so far?" It was impossible to interpret his low groan, so she tackled another subject. "Jody was awfully worried. He couldn't help thinking about what happened to Ken, you know? And he kept asking and asking, 'Where's Tate?' "

She turned the hall light on. He blinked and squinted like a man who'd just awakened.

"I'll go in and tell him I'm back. Would it be okay to wake him up?"

"I think it would be a good idea. I made him go to bed, but if he's asleep, he's probably not *sound* asleep, because there's that—" She touched his sleeve, pressed her lips together briefly and nodded. "That worry."

Tate nodded stiffly. She wanted to say what he wanted to hear, what she had not quite managed to claim—that it was her worry, too. He turned on his sock-clad heel and made his way down the hall. She listened for the low creaking sound she identified with Jody's door. Even with the bathwater running, she was able to tune in to their voices—one small and high, the other deep and comforting. Tears stung her eyes. She wiped them away quickly and made herself busy. Busyness kept sentimentality at bay.

"You were right," Tate said when he returned from his mission. "He was awake. I think I lost a few points with him when I told him I got lost. He says if Santa Claus brings him a real horse this year, he's goin' with me next time, because he knows the way home." He smiled as he tackled his shirt buttons. "I think that's a hint."

"I've heard it before. That broomstick is the only kind of horse Santa Claus is ever dropping down *this* chimney." She hand-tested the temperature of the water. "I'm surprised he didn't pounce on you the minute you walked in."

"He heard us whispering, and he couldn't make out who it was. He was afraid to come out and see." He pulled his shirttail free of his jeans. "Sometimes a little kid gets scared when he hears adults whispering. He's afraid something bad has happened." He shrugged as he unbuttoned his cuffs. "Or he *knows* something bad has happened, and he's afraid of what might come next."

"You're still talking about Jody?" she asked carefully. She remembered Ken telling her that Tate had lost his mother when he was a boy, but she knew nothing about the circumstances.

"Sure, Jody. Or any little guy." He shed the plaid flannel shirt and whisked his T-shirt over his head. "He thought maybe the sheriff was here."

"He remembers the last time I called the sheriff," she said absently. She was staring. Tate's chest seemed so much bigger now that it was bare.

"So now he knows it doesn't always end up like that." He unbuckled his belt and gave her a crooked smile. "You wanna stick around and wash my back?"

"I'm sorry. I didn't mean to keep…" It wasn't easy to tear her eyes away. "I want to get some hot food in you, and this is one time I wish I had some liquor in the house."

She supposed she had that sinister-sounding chuckle coming.

He supposed turnabout chest-ogling was fair play.

"I think there's a bottle downstairs with a genie named Jack inside who could grant you that wish." His favorite brand. He hadn't brought it in, but she didn't need to know that. He figured Kenny had left it right where Tate would find it, in a drawer in the gun cabinet, alongside the liniment and the Ace bandages.

"Then we'll break the seal and let the genie out." She waltzed out the door, adding cheerfully, "For medicinal purposes, of course."

"Of course."

The water burned like hell at first, even though he knew it wasn't that hot. But he closed his eyes and rubbed it over him, letting it do its work. He didn't see any sign of frostbite, which was good, but restoring his circulation was a painful process.

"Tate?" It was Amy's voice, calling out just above a whisper. "I brought you something to put on. Ken's things. Is that okay?"

"Sure. The door's unlocked." He slid the shower door closed. "There. I'm behind glass. Just set it inside."

But she came into the room. "I found your genie, too."

"The one in the gun cabinet?"

"You and Ken must think alike. I mean, the two of you must *have thought* . . ."

"Like two pups in a basket, in some ways." Through the opaque glass he could see her, an obscure shape in a white robe, hanging some sort of reddish stuff on a hook on the back of the door. "Maybe we're still on the same wavelength. I knew right where to look."

"So did I." She gave a small laugh as she left the room, closing the door softly behind her.

After he toweled off, he debated with himself about putting his own clothes back on. It bothered him that the maroon terry-cloth robe smelled like somebody else's shaving lotion. And plaid flannel pajamas. He never wore pajamas. He figured for the sake of decency he ought to put on the pants, but the hell with that shirt. He couldn't believe Kenny had worn such a thing to bed. The sheepskin slippers were pretty dudish, too, but they were warm.

Tate tied the belt on the robe and checked himself out in the mirror. He needed a shave, but his razor was downstairs, and he didn't want to use the shaving cream in the medicine cabinet. He didn't like the smell of that, either. It wasn't his brand.

He shuffled into the kitchen and enjoyed having Amy wait on him at such a late hour. Beef stew and homemade bread warmed his shivering insides. Her robe was similar to his—or Kenny's—but hers was long and white. He wanted her to sit down with him without having to ask her to, but she kept bouncing in and out of the room.

Then he heard a crackling sound in the living room, and he turned to find her standing in the doorway and looking strangely hesitant. "Would you like to sit by the fire for a while?"

"Not alone."

"No." She watched him wash his soup bowl. "I'll have to feed the baby soon anyway."

He glanced at the clock.

"A couple of hours," she amended.

"A shot of whiskey and a warm fire would do me just fine, then."

He pushed the sofa closer to the fire. She poured him a shot of whiskey. She even warmed it over a flame before she handed it to him. "Dr. Jack," he said as he raised his glass to the fire.

"Was there water in the stock tank?" she wondered as she joined him on the sofa.

"I ran the pump."

"And how about the barn? And did you open the door to the shed in the far pen, in case—"

"I opened the door."

"I should have put fresh straw—"

"I put down fresh straw." He glanced askance at her. She was back to testing him. "I took care of it, Amy."

"I wasn't sure you'd think of—"

"I damn near froze my tail off getting your sheep back to the fold, lady. You think I'm gonna leave the job half done?"

"No."

She turned quietly to watch the fire, and he watched the firelight burnish her face while the flames danced in her eyes. He sipped his drink and toyed with the thought of going to bed with her. Not seducing her. Just getting up off the sofa when the time came and going to bed with her, as if he were her man.

"You think nobody else can do it quite as good as Amy can," he observed flatly.

"I couldn't have..." The words got stuck in her throat.

"Go on." He waited, then coaxed with a gesture. "You couldn't have what?"

"Well, I probably couldn't have—"

"Uh-uh, it was better the other way." He smiled, enjoying her struggle. "Come on, now, I worked hard for this."

"I couldn't have done any better myself."

"Damn right you couldn't have. I froze my—"

"I know, and I do appreciate that special sacrifice."

"I fed them and watered them and tucked them in for the night. I was gonna sing to them, but they said not to bother. They'd heard enough of that on the way home. On the way *back*." He drained his glass, and she poured him a refill in what he figured to be her bottom-line show of appreciation. "Hell, I don't even like sheep, and here I am, treatin' 'em like—"

"Children?"

"Cattle." He had half a mind to push his luck and light up a cigarette. "I'm a cowboy, remember?"

"I remember." She set the bottle on the hearth and studied it for a moment. "And I remember how I used to treat you after I married Ken."

"You always invited me to stay for supper. I always knew I could bunk in here for a night or two as long as I wasn't raisin' any hell." He smiled, remembering. "If Kenny and me went out and tied one on, I knew better than to set foot in your kitchen. I didn't blame you for that."

"You always saw that he got home."

"This was where he belonged. He had somebody waitin' for him."

"In most ways he was a very good husband. He didn't spend much time in the bars, except . . ."

"Except when I was around. Right?" She didn't have to answer. She was still staring at the bottle. "You know why married women are always tryin' to fix the single guys up and get 'em married off?" She shook her head. "They think their husbands envy our freedom. And maybe they do sometimes."

"They probably do."

"But it works both ways. We envy them, too, sometimes. Like when it's time to go home." He laid his arm along the back of the sofa and leaned closer, changing his mind about the cigarette. He liked the fresh scent of her hair. "How come you never tried to fix me up with somebody, Amy? Why weren't you introducing me to your sister? 'Fraid I'd ruin her?"

"My sister is older," she said evasively. "She was already married."

"A friend, then. Somebody just like you."

"It wouldn't be fair. You only want a home *sometimes*, Tate. Like when you're cold and tired."

He wasn't listening. "You don't have any friends just like you." He touched the softly curling ends of her hair. "There aren't any more like you, Amy. I've looked."

She looked at him skeptically. "Where?"

"Church socials. PTA meetings. Choir concerts."

"Don't you mean truck stops, rodeos and bars?"

He grinned lazily. "Don't tell me I'm lookin' for love in the wrong places."

"Don't tell me you're looking for love."

"Just lookin' for comfort tonight," he said lightly. "A warm fire and a hot meal." He sipped his whiskey, thinking maybe there was some kind of love to be found somewhere in the whole combination.

The baby's soft cry from the back room made him smile again. "Sounds like I'm not the only one." He caught Amy's hand as she started away. "You comin' back?"

"I'll bring her in here."

He poured himself another drink, resettled himself on the sofa and watched the sparks sail up the flue while he waited.

"I had to change her completely," Amy explained when she came back with the baby. "She was soaked through."

"Thought maybe you'd gone shy on me and decided to stay in the bedroom."

Baring her breast, she held his gaze with eyes that said she kept her promises. She'd promised to sit next to him while he warmed himself with fire and whiskey. And now she warmed him with a special intimacy.

"I like to watch you feed her. I haven't spent much time around babies. Or mothers feeding babies this way." He set his glass down and leaned over Amy's shoulder to watch the busy little mouth. "Not human mothers, anyway."

A feeling of possessiveness surged through him, and he wanted to physically become a shelter around this little family so that he could keep it safe from the cold night. He cupped his big weather-roughened hand over the baby's tiny head. Her downy hair felt precious and delicate against his palm. He remembered his first glimpse of it, what a wet, sticky, welcome and glorious sight the top of this little head had been, and it occurred to him that he'd put the cart before the horse. He had never made love to Amy, but in a sense he'd given her this child. He hadn't planted the seed, but he'd delivered the baby into her arms.

Little Karen drank herself to sleep, which was what Tate thought he would do, right there in front of the fire, after Amy took the baby back to bed. But Amy came back and sat beside him, as though it were her place. He tried not to think about the fact that he was wearing Kenny's robe, which smelled like Kenny's after-shave.

"You have a wonderful way with Jody," she told him. "I don't know whether I've mentioned that."

"No, you haven't."

"You seem to know all the right things to say. He's had to grow up a lot these past few months. He's been my strong little man."

"He still needs time to be your little boy. I'm not sayin' you don't do right by him, because you do. And you've had a lot on your mind. It's just that—" He shook his head. He knew he had to be half-shot if he was coming up with advice about raising kids. But she was looking at him as though she thought *he* thought she'd done something wrong, so he had to explain. "Sometimes when you get a new baby in the house, the older kid gets to feelin' like a milk bucket sittin' under a he-goat."

"While the mean old nanny—"

"Now, I didn't say that at all." He drew a deep breath and sighed. "And I don't wanna be buttin' into your business. I especially don't wanna be buttin' heads with you right now. I might crack."

"So enough about goats?"

"Enough about goats," he agreed. He dropped his hand on his thigh and rubbed his palm against the terry cloth. "I've got no right to talk, anyway, after the way I got after the little fella the day I was unloading hay."

Amy touched the back of his hand. "How old were you when your mother died, Tate?"

"Ten." He wasn't sure where that question had come from, but her touch would be his undoing. He could tell that right now. "She had some kind of routine surgery—gall bladder, I think—and there were complications. But I was almost grown. It wasn't like

Jody, losing his dad before he even had a chance to—"

"Ten is hardly almost grown."

"When you live on a ranch, it is. The gospel according to Oakie Bain says that twelve is old enough to do a man's work." He turned his palm to hers, and their fingers seemed to lace together of their own accord. "All I'm saying is, just don't rush it. It'll happen soon enough. Once you give him a man's responsibilities, he won't be a boy anymore. And there's no such thing as a *little* man."

"You had a younger brother, didn't you?" He turned his face to the fire. "Ken told me."

"He told you what happened?"

"He said that your brother was killed in a farm accident when he was quite young. That's what you're thinking about, isn't it?"

"I'm talking about Jody." He tried to shrug it off. "Just making a simple observation. Take a look at it, or leave it alone."

"I'll take a hard look at it, Tate. It's a lot more than a simple observation." She paused, but it was too late to step back. "What was his name?"

"Jesse." His voice became distant, alien, drifting in desolation. "My brother's name was Jesse. Half brother. Oakie was his father, not mine." That was enough, he told himself. She'd only asked for his name. But his mouth wouldn't be still. "Jesse was only nine years old. By anybody's standards, that's still a boy."

"What happened?"

"I backed over him with the tractor." Damn the whiskey and damn his thick tongue. "Ran a 4020 just like yours right over his . . . right over him." He heard the catch in her breath. She didn't need any more details. "I figured Kenny must've told you the whole story."

"No." She squeezed his hand, and he could feel the pressure in the pit of his stomach. "Can *you* tell me?"

"I just did. I killed him. That's all she wrote."

"But it was an accident," she assured him softly.

"It was a crazed tractor," he countered. "One like you read about in a horror novel." With a look, she questioned his judgment. He studied the contents of his glass as he recalled some of his best recriminations. "Or else it could have been a booby trap that some prowler set to trip Jesse up. Or an earthquake sort of threw us both off balance. Anything but an accident. Accidents happen when people get careless."

"How old were you?"

"Twelve." He gave a long, hollow sigh. "I remember it like it was last night's dream. Real vivid, you know, but just beyond your grasp. Just past the point where you can turn it around and shake it up and make some sense out of it. All you can do is let it play itself out. You open your mouth to scream, and nothing comes out. You watch yourself slam on the brake, and you see the look on Oakie's face, and he's waving his arms. Is he saying go forward? Go back? And you get that awful, sick feeling all over again when you realize your brother's under the tire."

He saw it all again in slow motion, for the umpteen-hundredth time. His hands were shaking, foiling his attempts to make the throttle work, to find the gear that would change the course of more than the tractor. He didn't see Oakie coming, and suddenly he was trying to turn a fall into a jump, then scrabbling out of the way. That was when he glimpsed Jesse's brown hair, and the outstretched hand, and the blood, just before he buried his own face in the alfalfa stubble and tasted dirt and bile and tears.

He felt untouchable, the way he always felt when he remembered, the way he had felt that day. He remembered thinking they would put him in jail, which was where he belonged. But instead, the sheriff had asked Oakie all the questions, sparing Tate a glance once in a while as Oakie had given the awful answers. "Is that right, son?" the sheriff kept saying. Tate didn't know; he'd just stared at his useless hands and nodded. His whole worthless body had gone numb. And no one had tried to touch him then.

But Amy touched him now. He wasn't sure what had happened to his drink, or what he'd said last. Suddenly Amy was holding both of his hands. He hated the way they were shaking. "One minute he was playing with a spotted pup Oakie had given him," Tate said distantly. "The next he was underneath the damn tire."

She bowed her head and pressed the back of his hand to her cheek. "You saw him, didn't you?" she whispered. "You found him broken and bleeding, the same way..."

The same way Kenny had been when she'd found him. Another shared intimacy. They knew the same nightmares.

"It wasn't your fault, Tate."

"How do you know?"

"You were only twelve years old," she reminded him. "Still a child yourself. You didn't kill your brother. It was a terrible—"

"Accident," he recited. "Tragic accident, horrible accident. I hate the word. It grates on my ears like somebody grinding his teeth." He watched the fire. "The sheriff said it was an accident. The neighbors, when they brought over their hot dishes and offered to help with the chores, they called it an accident. Oakie didn't say much of anything, not for a long time. Kids from school said, 'Sorry about what happened, Tate' and that was that. Nobody talked about it much after we buried Jesse. Or if they did, they talked around it."

"It's always in the back of your mind when you farm," Amy said quietly as she rubbed her thumbs over the backs of his hands. "You like to think it's a good way to raise kids. And it is. You want them to take part in the work because it builds character, and they learn so much."

She closed her eyes, and a lone tear slipped down her cheek. She shifted a little, hoping he hadn't seen it. "But there are the accidents. They happen, Tate. They happen more often than most people want to realize. They happen with adults at the controls. You were only—"

"A boy?" He shook his head. "I was doing a man's job. I was expected to act like a man. Stand up like a man. Own up to my mistakes like a man, meaning you don't make excuses and you keep your blubbering to yourself." He was quoting now, almost verbatim.

"You weren't allowed to—"

"Cry? No way. Not unless I wanted Oakie to, uh—" He recalled his stepfather's favorite warning. "Give me something to cry about. The only person I ever talked to about it was Kenny, and that was only after I'd had a few drinks, like now." Still staring into the fire, he gave a humorless smile. "Ol' Kenny and me, we learned to act like men. Drank and smoked like men. Cussed and scrapped it out like men. Chased us some girls and had us some women, just like real men."

With a groan she tried to be subtle about drying her cheek on her own shoulder. "Now you're beginning to sound like the other Tate."

"What other Tate?" He took her chin in his hand and made her look at him. "There is only one Tate Harrison."

"Maybe so." She took a deep, steadying breath. "But he has an outside and an inside."

"Just like everybody else." He found the dampness on her cheek with his finger.

"You've worked hard at toughening up the outside. You've done a better job than anyone I know. But when the chips are down, you always come through. You'd go out drinking, and Kenny was always the one who got plastered. You were the one who brought him home. You were always watching out for him."

His mouth quirked slightly as the knowing smile flashed in his eyes. "Hornin' in on your territory?"

"He was my husband."

"Kenny had his head in the clouds most of the time, but he didn't worry much since he had us both watchin' out for him." He raised one brow. "Trouble is, he got away from us one night. And you've been thinkin' you should've gotten to him sooner, while I've been thinkin' I should've been here."

"Crazy, isn't it?"

"It'll drive you crazy. Believe me, I know."

"I want Jody to be...different. I don't want him to *act* like a man. I want him to *be* a man. Independent. Responsible."

"Like his mom?" She was all set to take exception, but he laid a finger against her lips. "Relax a little. Let him be a boy first. I told you about Jesse because..." The name came hard, as always, but this time he had Amy's hand in his, and her acceptance. "Because of Jody."

Which wasn't the whole of it, and she knew that as well as he did, but it was easier to advocate for the boy. "He watches you with the baby," he said, remembering, looking down at their clasped hands, now lying in her lap. "I told him how the baby wasn't going to be much fun for a while, and he's trying hard to understand all that, but he needs—" She looked up, and he looked into her eyes and said almost inaudibly, "He needs you to hold him."

"I can do that," she said gently. He leaned closer, and she put her arms around him and laid her cheek against his chest.

A man's need to touch a woman was a given, but the need to be touched by her was something else. He felt the need so strongly, he was almost afraid to return the gesture, afraid he would give himself away.

They wouldn't touch him. He'd done an awful thing, and nobody wanted to touch him.

"This isn't what I learned about acting like a man," he said as he slid his arms around her. He closed his eyes and nestled his face in her hair. "Hangin' on to you for dear life like this."

"Is that what you're doing?"

He didn't think he could hold her close enough, but she found a way to surround him with more warmth than the fire in the hearth radiated. He breathed deeply of the sweet strawberry-and-smoke scent of her. "I feel like the kid who got lost in the woods. It sure was dark out there."

"Could you use a kiss, too?"

"Not the kind you'd give to a kid."

She slid her fingers into his thick hair and pulled his face down to hers, kissing him as hungrily, as greedily, as fervently, as he'd ever been kissed. He'd never wanted anything more desperately than he craved her touch right now, but not if he had to ask. And he didn't. Suddenly her hands were all over him under the robe, caressing his hair-spattered chest, his shoulders, his flat nipples. He sucked in a deep breath and offered her access to his belly. He was on his way to heaven when she touched him there.

He untied the sash and drew the robe back, trying to shrug out of it without changing her course. "This thing smells like somebody else, Amy." Her fingertips curled into his waist, and she went still. He dropped his head back against the sofa. "Is that what you want?" he demanded quietly. "You want me to be somebody else?"

"No." She pressed her forehead against his chest and breathed soft words on his skin. "God help me, no."

"I want you so bad. You know that, don't you?" She nodded against him. "But I'm not Kenny. I don't own a robe and slippers. I don't wear pajamas. I'm not—" He couldn't be, not even if he had the heart to try, and she had to accept that. "I don't ever want you to call me by the wrong name."

She sighed. "Tate, I know who you are." She lifted her head and met his gaze. "I'm beginning to, anyway. You're the man who delivered my baby, the man who fixed my son's broomstick horse, the man who—"

He touched his finger to her lips. He didn't want her gratitude. "I want to make love to you."

"It's too soon."

"Because of the baby?" He searched the depths of her eyes for her answer. "Or because of Kenny?"

"Both," she admitted. She closed her eyes against the disappointment she saw in his. "Both."

He nodded and withdrew.

"That doesn't mean we can't give each other—" She extended her hand to him quickly, then closed it on a second thought. "I started to say 'what *we've* been giving.' But you've been giving, and I've been taking."

"It hasn't been easy, has it?" She looked at him, perplexed. "Taking help from Tate Harrison."

"Oh, Tate," she said as she took him back in her arms.

It had been *too* easy. Too quickly she had come to rely on him. Too readily she had let him lay claim to a too-large piece of her heart. She'd made it all too obvious. She hugged him, but she gave him no more of an answer. At least she could try not to show him *how* readily and *how* easily and *how* much.

He kissed the top of her hair and held her close. "It hasn't been easy givin' it, either."

Chapter Eight

Thanksgiving seemed to creep up overnight, but it did not pass without a traditional dinner. Tate was invited to carve the turkey and sit at the head of the table. He obliged. Even though he hardly considered himself a jack of the turkey-carving trade, he figured it out without asking for any pointers. Sitting in Kenny's chair at feast time felt a lot like wearing Kenny's robe and slippers, which Tate had quietly returned to the bedroom closet and never worn again. The prospect of an opportunity to play Santa Claus would have held considerable appeal except for the idea of filling someone else's boots again. Tate had his own boots. They were broken in nicely and fitted him just fine.

Amy hadn't been into town since the horse sale. The roads were icy, and she was glad when Tate volunteered to drive her in for the requisite six-week checkup. She had to take Jody along for a throat culture, and he and the baby were both fussy. The waiting room at the rural clinic was packed with whining children and cranky mothers. Tate excused himself to do some errands and promised to meet Amy and the kids at the Big Cup Café, two doors down the street.

It bothered her to find him sitting at a booth with her sister-in-law and Patsy Drexel. Marianne was working her way through a club sandwich, and Tate and Patsy were sharing a laugh and a cigarette. She was just passing it back to him, and he was about to take a drag when he saw Amy. One quick puff and, to his credit, he put it out before she brought the children to the table.

Patsy eyed the ashtray regretfully, as though she hadn't gotten her fill. Too bad, Amy thought.

"You guys ready for lunch?" Tate tipped his hat back and smiled. "I've been waitin' to order."

Amy shook her head. "We can wait 'til we get home. I have plenty of—"

"Mom, can I have a hamburger?" Jody pleaded.

"You can sit right up here with me and have anything you want, partner." Tate reached over the backrest and nabbed a booster seat from the empty booth on the other side. "We're too hungry to wait, aren't we? How's your throat?"

"They stuck a stick down it." Jody demonstrated with his forefinger. "Yech!"

"What you need is a big, fat hamburger and maybe some hot—" Tate glanced at Amy "—soup? Some orange juice?"

A little late to be asking my opinion, Amy thought. Jody had already scrambled into the booster seat, which Tate had pulled close to his side. She sighed and nodded, eyeing the remaining space on the horn of the half-moon booth. "Whatever he orders will be hard for him to swallow, and it's coming out of your wages, Harrison."

"That's all right," he said, chuckling as he signaled waitress Madge Jensen. "I've been meaning to suggest a pay cut, anyway. The seconds are killing my boyish figure."

Marianne offered to hold the baby, and Patsy spared the bundle a cursory glance as Amy wearily took a seat. She felt as though she'd just been to the doctor for anemia and he'd prescribed leeches. The bill—like all bills these days—had been higher than she'd expected. It worried her that she hadn't been able to pay it in full. She needed the cup of tea Tate suggested. She *wanted* the lunch he offered that she wouldn't have to prepare herself.

"We need anything from the store?" Tate asked.

The question surprised her. Tate had been picking up milk and eggs when he went to town, and he knew how well stocked her freezer and pantry were with her own produce. Now that she was doing the cooking again, she made everything from scratch. No more canned soup.

"Thought maybe I could take you grocery shopping." He sipped his coffee, then offered a teasing grin. "Wouldn't that be fun?"

Compared to what? Amy wondered. Delivering babies? All the fun things he could do with Patsy?

"I don't have my coupons with me." She glared at him. *How do you like that for mundane?*

"Amy and her coupons." Marianne chortled. "Bill, Sr., never had to bother with coupons and weekly specials until Amy moved in and started talking it up. But since our store is a franchise..." She smiled sweetly. "Well, we went along with it, so everything's up-to-date in Overo now. I just don't see where you find the time to mess with all that stuff, Amy. Clipping coupons and watching for bargains."

"I'm organized," Amy said dryly. A quick glance at Tate forced her to add, "Usually. And I don't buy what I don't need."

"What do you need for lunch?" Tate's nod turned her attention to the waitress, who was standing near Amy's shoulder, pencil and pad ready.

"Just a glass of water, please, Madge."

"You are the stubbornest woman I've ever known," Tate grumbled under his breath after he and Jody had put in their orders.

"I'll have to agree with that," Marianne put in. "Have you given any more thought to having a geological survey done? Tobart Mining is still interested."

Tate tucked his cigarettes into his jacket pocket. "They've approached me, too."

"What are *you* going to do?" Marianne asked.

"I don't know." He picked up his coffee cup. "I've been thinking about selling out altogether. If I do, I guess I'll hang on to the mineral rights."

"So in a year or two I'm likely to be looking at a strip mine right down the road," Amy surmised with blatant disgust.

"Just because you let them take core samples doesn't mean you're asking for strip mining."

"Really?" The look she gave him was cold enough to freeze beer. "What do you think they'll find in our basin, Tate? Gold nuggets?"

"Well, there could be oil, natural gas. There could be a lot of things." He dismissed the possibilities with a disinterested shrug. "They reclaim the land."

"We're ranchers." Amy turned to her husband's sister. "That was all Ken ever wanted. A working ranch."

"I think you mean a working *wife*," Marianne said. She shifted the baby to her shoulder. "Ranches don't work. *People* work. And you work too hard, Amy."

That was her choice. "Your father left Ken his land and you his money." *Mine gave me a strong back.*

"I also own half the mineral rights."

"Which are useless to you unless I agree to exploration. The land is Ken's legacy to his children," Amy said firmly. "It won't be mined. Now, can we talk about something else, please?" She offered a tight smile as Madge appeared with coffee refills. "I believe I will have a cup of tea and a BLT, Madge. Are you ready for Christmas, Marianne? How about you, Patsy? Have you done all your shopping?"

"I've done some," Patsy drawled. She glanced Tate's way and sighed. "Seems like I'm always shopping around."

* * *

Amy had turned the heat down before she left, and the house was cold. Almost as chilly as the attitude she had given him since they'd left the café, Tate thought. It couldn't have been over the comment about stopping at the store. Hadn't she been the one wishing aloud for some fresh fruit just the other day? Besides apples, she'd said. She had apples in the pantry.

He wasn't just sure what he'd done, but he figured it had to do with Patsy Drexel. If that were the case, he could afford to feel a little smug, considering his innocence. He went about his business, feeding the livestock, mending a hasp on one of the gates and sneaking his morning's purchases down to his room when everyone was napping. He was feeling pretty damned organized, too, now that he'd done some Christmas shopping. He'd never wrapped a Christmas present in his life, and he'd thought about leaving the stuff with Marianne or Patsy, along with a hint that he hadn't used a pair of scissors since he was in grade school. But he'd missed his chance.

The gun cabinet had obviously been one of Kenny's places for secreting things. Since Amy hadn't disturbed Kenny's whiskey stash or checked the guns, Tate took the cabinet to be property left untended, now that its owner was gone. It wouldn't hold everything he'd bought, but there was plenty of room for the things he didn't want Amy to find. He heard her footsteps on the stairs just in time to shut the door and lock it.

"Another drink to warm up?"

He didn't know why the question stung him. He'd thought about it himself, actually, but he'd changed his mind. He didn't like the way she was standing in the shadows at the foot of the stairs and looking at him like he was some kid who ought to know better. Maybe he'd just change his mind back again.

She wagged her head and sighed disgustedly. "Ken always thought he was so clever. If you insist on having it in the house, you might as well keep it in the kitchen and use a glass."

"What's left from Ken's stock *is* in the kitchen. I just needed a place to stash a few things under lock and key." Working hard to keep his cool, he bounced the key in his hand for her benefit. "The lock doesn't do much good with the key sittin' right in it."

Slowly she walked over to the gun cabinet, stared at the glass door for a moment, then ran her hand over the carved molding. "It's been a slow process, dealing with Ken's things—his drawers, his side of the closet, his boxes and boxes of keepsakes. He never threw anything away." Her hand dropped to her side. "I haven't gotten to this yet, but the guns aren't loaded."

"The .22 pistol had two rounds in the clip."

"Oh, Ken." She drew a deep breath and cast her glance heavenward. "Why were you always so...?" With a quick shake of her head, she took the blame herself. "I should have thought to check. I should have been more careful."

"Everything's unloaded now. If you don't have any use for them, you could probably get a good price for some of them. Maybe keep one around for—"

"They're Jody's." She folded her arms and turned away from the cabinet. "They will be when he's old enough. Some of them belonged to Ken's father. One was his grandfather's." She stepped closer to Tate, distancing herself from the Becker family heirlooms. "Otherwise, I wouldn't have them around."

He wondered whether she'd ever told Kenny any of this. He remembered that the cabinet itself had been in Kenny's family forever, as had the love of guns. Tate owned a couple of hunting rifles, too. He figured most guys did.

"Out here alone, you've got predators to worry about, maybe prowlers." No surprise to her, he thought. If Kenny had been good for nothing else, he'd been capable of protecting what was his. "If you don't know how to use a gun, I can sure teach you."

"You're going to sell your land, aren't you, Tate?" The question came out of left field. He missed the catch, so she pitched her charge again. "You're just going to sell out to the highest bidder."

Was she kidding? For years the bidding had been closed to anyone but Kenny. "I've only kept it this long because Kenny wanted it. When you guys dropped the lease, I kinda figured—"

"It's been in your family. It belonged to your father."

"Yeah, well, he died young because he worked too damn hard. He had a bad heart. This is no life for a man with a weak heart." He thought better of adding, *Or a woman with two little kids.* "That's about all I know about him, too. He died when I was even younger than Jody."

Damn, he was at it again, spilling personal history like a leaky washtub.

"Jody won't remember much about his father, either, but he'll have the home his father left him."

"Forever and ever, amen?"

"A home is important." She jabbed his shirt button with her forefinger. "Roots, Tate. Roots are important. They give you a strong sense of who you are."

"You have a strong sense of who *you* are." He closed his hand around hers. "You've only lived here since you married Kenny. Where are your roots?"

"They're here. They grew fast, once they had fertile ground."

"Like the tree you fed from your own womb?" He didn't realize he was going to take her shoulders in his hands until he felt their slightness. "Aren't you afraid this land might suck the life right out of you, maybe through those roots you put down?"

"No," she said, standing her ground without pushing him away, as he might have expected. "I've brought new life here. I've made a home. A permanent home. You sold your family's house, and now you're going to sell the land it sat on."

"I don't have any use for it."

"They'll rape it, Tate. The speculators, the investors, the miners. They'll strip it down and violate it."

A caustic comeback sprang to the tip of his tongue, but he couldn't quite spit it out. He couldn't accuse her of being melodramatic, not with that look on her face and the image that the word *rape* brought to his mind. It was more than a risk to the land. It was a threat to Amy, to her power to make life flourish, to the essence of her femininity. In her eyes he revisited her pain and her triumph in the moment she'd given birth.

"You want it?" he demanded flippantly. The life force burned so strongly in her eyes that he was forced to turn away. "Take it," he said, his bravado deflating. "Christmas present, free and clear. I'll sign over the title."

"Don't be ridiculous," she tossed back.

He turned like a cornered gunfighter, the words piercing him as sharply as any bullet could have. "You've said that to me before, Amy. Remember?" *Remember the night I drove you home? You made your choice that night.* "'Don't be ridiculous, Tate.'"

She stared, frowning slightly, trying to dredge up some recollection of the details in her mind. Clearly it wasn't an easy task for her. Maybe it wasn't much of a memory for anybody but Tate.

"There was no way I was gonna hang around this town after you married Kenny and set up your *permanent* housekeeping with him. *That* would have been ridiculous."

"So you chose to live like a gypsy."

"A cowboy," he corrected with a cocky grin. "Don't gypsies raise *sheep?*"

"I don't know. All I know is that they wander from place to place, and their children just—" she gestured expansively "—wander with them."

"I don't have any children, so what difference does it make how I choose to live my life?" His eyes challenged her. He folded his arms and braced his shoulder against the gun cabinet. "What difference does it make to *you,* Amy. Why should you give a damn?"

"You were my husband's friend."

"It has nothing to do with Kenny, and you know it. It has to do with you and me, and it always has."

"There was no 'you and me.' You weren't really—"

His hand shot out and grabbed her shoulder again. "The only thing I wasn't really was the kind of man you were looking for. You chose your husband carefully, didn't you?"

She stiffened. "Yes, and you were his friend, which made you *our* friend."

"Give me a break." With a groan he released her and turned away, patting his empty shirt pocket. His cigarettes must have been in his jacket. It was about time for a smoke and the drink she'd first accused him of sneaking.

But at his back, she persisted with her crusade. "You know, you could have built something on that land instead of tearing down what was left and going off—"

Great suggestion. "You would have enjoyed that, would you?" He confronted her again, trying hard not to sneer. "You married to Kenny, and me living just down the road?"

"It wouldn't have bothered me."

"Yeah, right. Well, it would have bothered the livin' hell out of me."

"I just meant that…" They stood face-to-face, but they were talking past each other. Intentionally. He knew what she meant, and he could tell by the look in her eyes that she knew damn well what *he* meant.

She shook her head and softened her tone. "You don't understand about the land because you've never been one to settle down. It's just not in you."

"I understand something about the land, Amy. I grew up here." He glanced away. He didn't like that soulful look she was giving him. "I guess I don't understand about the roots. Mine must have eroded. What was left after Jesse died was me and Oakie. Two people who tolerated each other. Barely."

"Why do you keep coming back, then?"

"To see Kenny." *What, was she blind?*

"Kenny's not here anymore."

"I'm stickin' around to help his wife and kids get through the winter."

"I'm his *widow*."

"Which means what? Besides the fact that you need a man?"

"I *don't* need a man!" Fingers rigidly splayed, she swept the idea away with an abrupt gesture, then calmly echoed, "I'm not talking about that. I'm saying you've come back to—"

"No, let's stop talking *around* it, Amy. I'm living under your roof, and Kenny's dead." He braced his arms on the gun cabinet, trapping her between them to keep her from turning away. "Several years ago you said it was wrong. Several cold nights ago you told me it was too soon. What are you tellin' me now?"

They stared at one another, and finally it was he who had to turn away. If he got hold of her again, he would begin trying to shake some sense into her. Or he would be kissing her senseless—one of the two. He sighed. "What do you want from me, Amy?"

"I haven't asked for anything."

"Doesn't it mean anything to you that you haven't *had* to?"

Her lips parted. He arched an eyebrow, waiting, but she pressed those lips together again. He gave a dry chuckle, as short on patience as she was on answers.

"I'm goin' out for a smoke," he told her as he headed for the stairs. "Call me when supper's ready. Whatever supper you think you can spare your hired *gypsy.*"

Tate thought a lot about "roots" when he and Jody rode into the hills—*his* hills, on his land—and selected a Christmas tree. He'd taken it as a somewhat positive sign when Amy hadn't refused to let Jody go along after Jody assured her that his throat wasn't "one bit sore anymore." The horseback part of the journey would be short, Tate had promised. They had trailered Outlaw as close in as they could. Then he'd put Jody in the saddle and mounted up behind him.

Maybe he did have some roots in the foothills, he thought. The huge, pale winter sky rose high overhead and slid down in the distance behind the snow-capped western peaks. The morning freshness was filled with sage and pine. It felt good to fill his chest with something besides smoke, to get himself light-headed on pure air.

"What we're gonna end up with is a juniper or a ponderosa pine. You think that's okay?" Tate wondered as he surveyed the snow-spattered red cuts and the flat-topped slopes.

Jody nodded vigorously, the bill on his little flap-eared plaid cap bobbing up and down like a barfly's eyelashes.

"They don't make the best Christmas trees, but we'll find a good one. We can't use a limber pine. See that one up there?" The boy nodded again. "The wind's turned it into a pretzel."

"Mom and me bought our tree last year," Jody reported. "Did your dad used to go cut your Christmas tree himself?"

"My stepdad did, yeah."

"Did he take you with him?"

"He did. This is where we'd always come lookin', too."

He remembered the year a bobcat had spooked the horses. Jesse had been just about Jody's age, and Tate and Jesse had been riding double. Their sixteen-hand palomino had laid his ears back, and they'd gone streaking across the flat, with Jesse hanging on to the saddle horn and Tate, mounted behind him, gripping the swells. He could still see that jackleg fence up ahead. Just when he'd thought they were goners, the big horse had sailed over the rails like a trained jumper and kept right on galloping until he wore himself out. Oakie's face had been whiter than the December snow cover, but he'd said he'd never seen any cowboy stick a horse better, and he'd been looking Tate straight in the eye when he'd said it.

"We always found a good one out here," Tate said, surprising himself as he echoed Oakie's annual pronouncement. "You can't get 'em any fresher."

They chose a small juniper. Even though it didn't have the pointed crown they were looking for, it had a straight trunk, and it was already decorated with cones that looked more like pale blue berries. Entrusted with Outlaw's reins, Jody was content to stand back and watch Tate cut the tree down. But the notion of roots bedeviled Tate as he swung the ax. He would take the tree away, but the roots would remain. If he came back to this spot years later, he knew he'd find juniper saplings. For every one that he pulled down, Amy would probably plant two more, with or without a placenta to nourish its roots. That was the way she was. A nester, like his mother, whose life had been hard and brief. His mother hadn't lived long enough to see the get of her womb reach manhood.

The tree went down, and Jody cheered. Tate straightened his shoulders and flashed a smile the boy's way. It was good for a boy to have a man to look out for him, too, Tate thought. And it was good for a man to remember that times weren't *all* bad when he was a boy.

Amy had been keeping to herself a lot lately, spending hours behind closed doors in the bedroom with the sewing machine whirring. The tree pleased her. She emerged long enough to give it her special homespun touch, adding brightly colored calico bows, along with small hanging pillows shaped like rag dolls and toy soldiers and teddy tears. She gave the top berth to a lacy angel, then stepped back and announced that she'd never seen a prettier tree.

After letting it be known that offers to entertain the baby would be more than welcome, Amy went back to her sewing machine. Tate and Jody discovered that Karen had an ear for harmonica music. Now that she could hold her head up, she liked to bob along with their songs.

After several hours of late-night work, Tate managed to get his packages wrapped. The paper was cut funny in places, and he'd had to use a lot of tape, but he felt good when he arranged the gifts under the tree. He'd saved all the receipts. Half the stuff probably wouldn't fit. The other half was probably purely frivolous, but he didn't care. He'd picked out things he wanted his . . . he wanted *them* to have.

Amy didn't say much when she saw all the packages, but Jody was bursting with excitement when he asked, rather cautiously, whether any of the packages might be for him. Tate pointed to his name on one of the tags and challenged him to find the others.

Jody found one small box to be especially fascinating. He kept checking it over, shaking it, staring as though he were trying to develop X-ray vision, and muttering his guesses as though the package might respond if he hit on the right word. By Christmas Eve he had almost become a fixture beneath the tree.

After a supper of what Amy called her Christmas Eve chowder, she disappeared into the bedroom one more time and emerged with an armload of packages and a broad smile. "I have some things to add to the booty," she told Tate as they met in the hallway.

"Can you use some help?" Karen had fallen asleep in his arms, and he'd just put her down in the crib in her nursery. "Looks like you've been busy."

"You guys probably thought I was avoiding you these last couple of weeks. I wasn't." She let him take the top half of her pile of packages. "Mine are all homemade."

"Makes them more special."

"Jody's too young to see it that way. I know he's excited about your gifts, and I'm trying not to be an old Scrooge about it."

With a quick frown he questioned her choice of words.

"What I mean to say is, I'm sure you bought him the kinds of things a little boy wants for Christmas."

"I was a little boy again when I did my shopping. You don't begrudge me that, do you?"

"No." They stood across from each other in the narrow hallway, his armload of boxes touching hers. A big red bow grazed her chin. "I appreciate it. It's the first Christmas without Ken, and I dreaded it. But you're here, and I'm glad, and—" She shrugged. "I guess I feel a little guilty about being glad."

He groaned. "You are so full of—" With a soft chuckle he tipped his head back against the wall. "The word that comes to mind...well, you'd take it wrong."

"Baloney?"

"That's not right, either. I know how you feel. I miss Kenny, too. Maybe not the same way you do, but I miss him." He ducked a little closer to her ear, as though he was sharing a secret. "I think it's okay to be glad about some things at Christmas, and still be sad about others. And I'm glad I'm here.''

''Where would you be if you weren't here?''

''No place special.'' Probably hanging around Reno or Denver, or maybe working the holidays for some trucking outfit, but she was looking at him as though she thought he was sitting on the keys to some pleasure palace. ''That's the truth, Amy. No place anywhere near this special.''

Jody had fallen asleep under the tree. Quietly Tate set his armload of packages aside and knelt beside the boy. The colored lights from the tree cast a rainbow of soft hues over his soft blond curls and his sleeping-in-heavenly-peace face. The warm glow seemed to seep into Tate's skin, like the gleam of approval he'd been seeing in the child's eyes lately.

That was a gift, he realized. The best gift anyone had ever given him. Nobody had ever accepted him unconditionally, the way Jody did. He imagined himself claiming his gift from under the tree as he lifted Jody into his arms, carried him to bed and tucked him in.

Amy had a steaming cup of apple cider waiting for him when he came back to join her on the sofa. ''Homemade,'' she said as she watched him take a sip. ''But it doesn't have much kick to it.''

''I like it the way it is.'' He pressed his lips together, savoring the cinnamon flavor. ''Homemade.''

She nodded toward the packages under the tree. ''It's that small box that fascinates him, but I don't think it's sugarplums he has dancing in his head. What's in it?''

"A gift for him and a surprise for you."

"The day you don't surprise me will be a surprise, Tate Harrison. I hope you didn't go overboard."

"I didn't." Not as far as he was concerned. "Anyway, what's done is done, and you're long overdue for a few pleasant surprises. And I'm just the man who can provide them, because you don't expect much." He gave her a mischievous wink. "I can look pretty damn good just by taking some time off from being bad."

"I wouldn't say that."

"You wouldn't say I look good?"

"You look—" she gave him a pointed once-over "—the way you've always looked." The observation made him squirm a little, which made her laugh. "Truthfully, I've always thought you looked good even when you were being your baddest."

"Baddest man in Overo?"

"Sometimes. You know darn well you turn a lot of heads, cowboy. You always have."

"But not yours."

"You know better than that," she admitted. "But I've always managed to be fairly practical."

"*Very* practical."

"I'm certainly not going to be unrealistic about a cowboy whose pickup odometer turns over every year." She glanced away from him, her attention drawn to the lights on the tree. "I do hate to see you sell your land, though. Someday you might wish you had a familiar place to park that pickup."

"I'm familiar with a lot of parking places."

"So was my father." She sighed deeply, and the lights twinkled in her eyes like distant memories. "My family moved all the time when I was growing up. When people ask me where I'm from originally, I still get all flustered with the need to explain. I used to launch into a complete history, but I've learned to simply pick a place." Her wistful smile seemed almost apologetic. "Or just to say that I'm from here now, because I *am*. I really am."

"Permanently planted, I'd say." Slipping his arm around her shoulders seemed a natural gesture. "Was your father in the military?"

"He should have been, but that was probably one of the few things he didn't try. He never held a job very long. He got bored." His hand curved comfortingly around her shoulder as her voice drifted and became almost childlike. "And I was never in one school for more than a year. He left us one winter when my mother decided that the trailer court we were living in was going to be home." A deep breath and a quick toss of her head grounded her in the present again. "She's still there, in Florida."

"Smart woman. I wouldn't wanna leave Florida in the winter, either. Where was the ol' man headed?"

"Who knows? I haven't seen him since."

He started to drink his cider, but a word from a previous conversation nagged at him. "Would you call him a gypsy?"

"Among other things." She offered a knowing smile. "He was a rover. He was a jack-of-all-trades. He was a lovable man in his way."

"Would you say he was a dreamer?"

"Oh, yes, he was that."

He looked her in the eye. "You know, you married a dreamer, too."

"Ken was not at all like my father. He may not have been much of a businessman, but he gave his family a home." She shrugged. "I'm surprised my father didn't try cowboying. It would have suited him well, I think."

"It would suit me well, too." Suit him just fine, he thought, as he drew his arm back and cradled the warm mug in both hands. "Except that I've been stuck with a damn flock of sheep lately."

"You're not stuck with them." She bit her lower lip, and he knew damn well she was thinking up a good one. Without looking up, she said quietly, "You're free to leave anytime."

"I was just..." *Damn,* she was a tough nut to crack. "I've made up my mind to see you and the kids through the winter, and that's what I'm doin'. I'm not sellin' any land before spring, and I'm not in any hurry to hit the road." He slid her a hard glance. "Unless you want me to."

"I just don't want you to feel obligated."

"I don't. I've got nothin' better to do. Simple as that."

Simple, hell. They stared at the Christmas lights until he couldn't stand the silence anymore. It was loaded with complications.

"Can't think of any place I'd rather spend the winter than Montana, freezin' my damn—" He glanced at her, and he thought he detected the hint of a smile in her eyes. "I don't know anyone in Florida who'd put me up for the winter, do you?"

"Not a soul."

"Besides, it's Christmas." He reached for her hand. "I'm not goin' anywhere at Christmas."

"Peace to you, then, cowboy." She gave him a peck on the cheek and whispered, "And merry Christmas."

Chapter Nine

Jody didn't see Tate sitting at the kitchen table when he rode his broomstick horse into the living room on Christmas morning. Tate had already made coffee, and he was quietly biding his time as he sipped the first cup of the morning. Just waiting. He smiled to himself when he heard Jody's, "Whoa." There was a pause, and then, "Whoa! Mom! Tate! Hurry, come look!"

Tate hitched up his beltless jeans and poured coffee into a second cup, which he passed across the counter to Amy as she came around the corner carrying the baby against her shoulder. "Santa even made coffee this year?" she marveled with a sleepy smile. "What a guy."

"Special Christmas service for people who do two-o'clock feedings," Tate returned as he walked around her and touched the baby's cheek with one finger. "Happy first Christmas, little darlin'."

Eyes as big as saucers seemed to be asking him what all the fuss was about. "This is Christmas," he explained, sliding his finger under her soft baby chin. "Are you ready for all the excitement?" She bounced her head up and down over her mother's shoulder and rewarded him with a smile.

Her brother galloped onto the kitchen scene, waving both arms wildly. "Come on, you guys! Hurry!"

Amy gave a throaty, morning laugh that sent shivers down Tate's back. "There's nothing in there that's about to run away, Jody." On second thought she cast Tate a warning glance as they headed for the living room. "Better not be anything on the hoof."

"There might be a few little tracks on the roof, but no new livestock this time around."

"Look at me, Mom!" Jody bounced astride the small saddle Santa had left under the tree. A small gasp escaped his mother's throat. "Just my size. Maybe there's a little horse for me outside!"

"Santa always takes these things one step at a time," Tate said. "I know for a fact that he never brings live animals without Mom's permission." Amy's soft sigh of relief made him grin. "But Santa knows every cowboy needs a good saddle, just in case."

A soft-body baby doll that was bigger than Karen earned a discreet test squeeze from her mother. The fancy stroller that could be converted for half a dozen uses obviously pleased Amy, too. "Santa heard that the stroller Jody used was ready for retirement," Tate said.

"Santa's insight was remarkable this year." Amy lifted the padded seat out of the stroller frame. On the floor it became a handy infant seat with handles that also served as rockers. Karen settled into it comfortably and quietly watched her first Christmas morning unfold.

No one tore through the gift wrap faster than Jody. He announced what each gift was, barely able to contain himself as he pulled it out of the box. "Cowboy hat—thanks, Tate! Cowboy pajamas—thanks, Mom! Record player—thanks, Tate! Monkey with a button nose—thanks, Mom!"

Amy opened a box and lifted out the ruffled dress he'd picked for Karen. He blushed when she held up the frilly bloomers. "I liked the bows on it." He shrugged and sipped his coffee. "The one you made for her is prettier, though."

"This one is fancier." Amy's eyes glistened. "I love it, Tate. It's just darling."

"Well, see what you think of this," he said, urging her to open another box. He'd decided that a woman who'd just put aside her maternity clothes probably needed some pretty new things in her normal size, and he'd chosen a sweater, slacks, blouse and a down-filled jacket with fur trim on the hood.

"I saved the receipts in case there's something you don't like." He reached behind the sofa and pulled out a huge fruit basket, wrapped in red cellophane and tied with a green bow. "Except this. We're eatin' this."

"That's enough for an army!" It made him feel warm inside to hear Amy laugh so readily. "I like everything, but we'll see what you guys think about the clothes when I try them on. I can't even guess what size I am now."

"I don't know if the styles are right." Tate eyed her appreciatively and gave a slow smile. "But I'll bet you two oranges and a banana that I didn't mess up on your size."

"You sound awfully confident." Her smile was coy. "Did you seek expert advice?"

"Didn't need any," he drawled. "Got a damn good eye."

She ducked under the far side of the tree and delivered a gaily wrapped box into his hands. "There aren't any receipts for yours. About all I can alter is the fit."

He couldn't believe she'd made the Western shirt herself, with its piped yoke, pearlized snaps and crisply tailored collar and cuffs. And the plush royal blue robe she'd made was monogrammed with his initials and a tiny horseshoe. Tate smiled a little self-consciously as he tried the robe on over his T-shirt and jeans. He'd never been big on clothes to wear around the house, but he could see how it might come in handy for a guy who had a house to hang around in. He thought about breaking it in with his own brand of after-shave.

"Do you like the color?"

"It's a great color." It didn't look anything like Kenny's. "We knew you were busy back there, but we had no idea *how* busy. Did we, Jody? Ma'am, you sure outdid yourself on that sewing machine."

"I'll take that as the stamp of approval." Admiring the way it looked on him, she assessed the sleeve length and adjusted the fluffy lapels, smoothing her hands over them to make sure they lay just right over his robust frame. "Does it feel comfortable in the shoulders?"

"It fits great."

"I thought you'd like a pocket," she said.

With two fingers he traced the large *H* in the middle of the monogram. "How did you know my middle name?"

"I sneaked a peek at your driver's license."

"Picked my pocket, huh?"

"You're an easy mark," she said lightly. "You left your pants in the bathroom. But your license only says 'Tate C. Harrison,' so I'm still wondering what the *C* stands for."

"Carter," he said. "After my father."

Their eyes met briefly, exchanging myriad feelings neither dared name. He wanted to kiss her, long and hard. She wanted to put her arms around him and hug him in the new robe she'd made for him.

But she smiled and patted its single pocket. "This isn't made to hold cigarettes."

"What's it for?"

"I don't know." She gave him a saucy smile. "Maybe your billfold."

"I do like to keep that handy."

Amy sat on the floor next to the baby and tested out the rocker as she surveyed the colorful torn-paper chaos. "What was in that small box, Jody? Did I miss that?"

"Didn't open it yet," Jody said as he withdrew the last box from underneath the tree. "I was saving it."

"Well, let's see what it is." Tate's eagerness shone in his eyes as he watched Jody unwrap the gift.

"The harmonica." With wide eyes and a voice full of wonder, Jody took the instrument from the box. "The silver-and-black one."

"Is that yours, Tate?" Amy asked quietly.

"I have a couple of them," he said absently. He was busy cherishing the look in the little boy's eyes. "This is Jody's favorite. Right, partner?"

"Tate's gramma gave him this," Jody reported. "It was his grampa's."

"Oh, Tate—"

"Jody has a surprise for you." He gave an encouraging nod. "Go ahead, son."

The word *son* was out before Tate knew it was coming. Jody didn't seem to notice, and neither did Amy. She was too intent on listening to Jody play "Jingle Bells" and "Frosty the Snowman." Tate figured he'd only used the word because right now it suited the way he felt. He wasn't trying to take anybody's place. But he was just as proud of the boy's accomplishment as any father could possibly be.

By afternoon the snow was falling thick and piling up fast. By nightfall the wind had picked up. When Tate went out to the barn to put the sheep to bed, he found that the snowdrifts were getting bigger. He hadn't thought it possible, but the sheep were getting stupider. The shed was three-sided, and the solid wood doors on the barn had to be left open whenever the building was used for a sheep shelter. There were no deadlier conditions for sheep than moist air in close and closed quarters. He'd been meaning to build slatted doors for the barn, but he hadn't gotten around to it yet. Now the dumb beasts were huddled in every corner of the pens outside, and the drifts were mounting around them.

Daisy and Duke seemed to realize right off the bat that this was no time to play games with the cowboy, even if his signals were a little off the mark. They took the cue to drive every last woolly creature under a roof. Tate couldn't help marveling at the dogs' work. He vowed that the pair would feast on T-bones or soup bones, whatever he could rustle up from Amy's freezer. After supper they would be bunking in his room for the night. When the chips were down, the cowboy and the sheepdogs made a remarkable team.

Amy didn't object when the dogs stumbled in the back door with him, blown in on a big wind. He could tell she'd been waiting anxiously, just as she had the night he'd trailed the sheep back from his pasture. Not that he wanted her to worry, but there was something pretty nice about being met at the door.

"Visibility must be down to zero out there," he announced as he shooed the dogs down the basement steps to keep them from shaking snow all over the kitchen. "Ol' Daisy and Duke sure did earn their—"

"Where's Jody?"

The question slammed the brakes on Tate's heart. He stared dumbly.

"He's not in the house, Tate. I was ready to brain you for taking him outside in this, but..." She kept looking behind him, as though she expected the boy to appear at his heels. "He's not anywhere in the house."

"Get me the biggest flashlight you've got." Tate jerked the back door open and whistled for the dogs.

"I'll get dressed."

"You stay with the baby. We'll find him."

It was the kind of windy whiteout that spawned Western disaster tales, and the worst kind was about the child who slipped outside unnoticed and froze to death only yards away from the house. Galvanized by fear, Tate called out as he followed the fence line toward the pens, but the dogs bounded through the drifts in a different direction. They seemed to be headed for the machine shed.

With every inch in every direction turned completely to snow, there were no directions. There was no order, no sense to anything. A mere man was almost useless. The snow stung Tate's face as he followed the two canine tails, which were about all he could see. The flashlight probably wasn't penetrating more than a few feet, and the wind had his lung power beat all to hell. He had to trust the dogs' keener senses.

But when he ran smack into the chain-link fence surrounding their kennel, he cursed the dogs roundly. "I said find *Jody* you dumb sons of—"

"Here I am!"

Daisy and Duke were already digging the snow away from the doghouse door. Jody emerged like a snowball, tumbling into Tate's arms. He'd had the good sense to dress warmly, and he'd found a snug place to take shelter. Throat clotted with a burning flood of relief, Tate hugged him close. A whistle for the dogs was the only sound he could manage.

"He's okay," Tate announced as he came through the door again, his legs considerably less steady this time. "He was in the doghouse."

"In the doghouse?" Laughing and crying at once, Amy reached out like a desperate beggar and took the boy in her arms. She sat him on the kitchen counter and peeled his ice-coated scarf away from his face. She laughed again, relieved to uncover a cherry-red nose and quivering lips. "How was it in there?"

"Cold as ice," Jody blurted out.

"I guess one trip to the doghouse is enough for tonight." She took off his hat and combed her fingers through his matted curls. "Oh, Jody, I was so scared."

"M-me, too. I was worried about Tate. Th-thought I c-could help him get done with his chores f-faster." His teeth chattered. "I couldn't f-find the b-barn."

"You didn't know how bad it was out there, did you, partner?" Tate offered as he glanced anxiously at Amy.

The looks they exchanged over Jody's head acknowledged the internal mélange of emotion that defied words. Terror was slow to give way to complete, bountiful relief. Amy didn't know whether to scold her son or simply hug him to pieces, then do the same for his rescuer. Tate didn't quite know what to do with himself, either, other than to try to shake off most of the snow in the vicinity of the scatter rug by the back door. Amy handed him Jody's jacket, and he hung it on a hook next to his.

From the back room came Karen's call for her supper. One look in Amy's eyes and Tate knew that the woman had finally reached her limit, emotionally and otherwise. She couldn't stand the idea of coming apart in front of anyone. She needed a few moments to herself.

"I'll give Jody a bath while you feed the baby."

"Are you—" She pressed her lips together tightly and cupped Jody's cheeks in her hands. "Toes hurt?" she croaked.

Jody shook his head. "I just went out...'bout three or seven minutes ag-go."

"I don't think he was out too long," Tate said. "We'll go in the bathroom and get ourselves thawed out."

Amy nodded and fled to answer the baby's call.

Jody pulled one of his boots off and dropped it on the floor. "She's real mad, ain't she?" he asked quietly.

"*Isn't* she." The correction rolled off Tate's tongue as though teaching the boy proper English was something he did every day. Where had *that* come from? he wondered as he hunkered down to pick up the boot. Jody handed him the second one. "She's not really mad. She was afraid you were lost in the snow, and I was, too. It was a mistake to go outside, Jody."

"A bad mistake," the boy agreed.

"But it's not like you were being a bad boy. The rule is that you don't go outside without asking. Right?"

"She wouldn't have let me go."

"And now you know why." He set the boots by the back door, then turned with his big hands outstretched. "Come on up here, partner." They traded bear-and-cub hugs. "Oh, that feels good. A bath will warm you up just fine. I know that from experience. First you, then me."

But it was a couple of hours before Tate got his shower, and by then it wasn't quite as much of a treat. He'd said good-night to Jody and left him to make peace with his mom, who offered to read him three stories instead of the usual one long one or two short ones. Tate had used the little shower downstairs, trying not to use up too much hot water, in case Amy still wanted some, and he'd wrapped himself up in his brand-new bathrobe. Then he'd plunked himself down on the bed with a magazine and sat there listening to the wind whistling above the window wells.

Since he'd taken up residence with Amy and the kids, he'd made a point to limit his smoking to the great outdoors, but this was one night when he figured he'd earned a shot of whiskey and a cigarette. Trouble was, even though the whiskey felt good going down and the smoke steadied him some, it made him feel lonely.

It was Christmas, and here he was sitting on a single bed in the basement of the first place that had felt like home to him in one hell of a lot of years. It was *Christmas,* and he was indulging himself in two of his favorite vices. Big thrill. Daisy and Duke were curled up as close together as cloves on a Christmas ham, and Tate felt like a man who'd been relegated to the doghouse.

His blue mood didn't make much sense. This was the spare bedroom, after all. Hired hand or guest, this was where the Beckers had always put him up. It was comfortable enough, and he had his privacy. It didn't make sense that the four white walls made him feel so damn lonesome, not with Amy and the kids right up-stairs.

But he'd spent this Christmas on an emotional roller coaster. His head was spinning with a hundred joys and fears, and there was no such thing as sense. If truth be told, he would have to say he'd started losing touch with his faculties the day he'd knocked on Amy's door and offered her a hand.

Offered to *be* her hand, and for next to nothing. In lieu of flowers, just the way he'd planned, just as the obituaries always said. Hell, he'd turned himself into a living memorial. Now he was turning himself inside out, like the kid looking for one last piece of candy in his Christmas stocking.

Pathetic. He damn sure didn't need steel guitars whining in the background to put him in a melan-choly mood. But, then, he was a cowboy, and all a cowboy had to do was pour himself a drink and *think* lonesome. He finished his cigarette, tossed back the last of his drink, turned the light out, took his clothes off and crawled into bed.

Damn, those sheets were cold.

Three quiet taps on his door brought him up on one elbow.

"Tate?"

Just like a woman. She could smell smoke in the middle of a blizzard, and she'd come to give him hell about it. Man, she'd sure tiptoed down the steps qui-eter than a feather duster.

"I'm . . . here."

The door opened slowly, and there she stood in her nightgown, backlit by the light in the stairwell. "The kids are in bed, and it's so quiet upstairs," she said in a small, shy voice. "I . . . well, I thought . . . the lights look pretty on the tree, and . . . it *is* nice and quiet." She paused, obviously waiting for him to jump at the chance to go up and sit with her. "I guess you're tired."

"Yeah," he said finally. "I'm tired." Seeing the way her shoulders sagged slightly brought him a small surge of satisfaction. Minute, actually, compared to the surge of hot current that was suddenly running strong and lusty through his body and heading straight for his lightning rod.

Amy stepped back as though she'd felt the shock. She was about to retreat just as quietly as she'd come.

He turned over on one hip. "Amy?" She paused. He could almost hear her misgivings, but he could see they weren't strong enough to take her away. She was caught in the balance.

"Amy, you gotta know that I'm down here bunkin' in the same room with two wet dogs who are huggin' each other up somethin' fierce, and my nerves are wound tighter than a spring, and I'm thinkin' if I could just get close to you right now . . ."

She went to him. Drifted across the floor like an apparition and knelt beside his bed. He swung his legs over the side of the bed and sat up, pulling the sheet over his lap. "Honey, I don't wear . . . any kind of pajamas."

"I noticed you were uncomfortable in them before."

"Amy, what I'm trying to tell you is I can't—" With her back to the dim light, he couldn't see her face. He could smell that strawberry soap she always used, and he forgot all about wet dogs. He took her face in his hands, touching the soft contours of her cheeks with his thumbs. "I want you so bad, I can hardly..."

"Hardly what?" She slid her hands over his upper arms, caressing hard muscle. "What would you be doing if you could get close to me tonight?"

"I'd be lovin' you up so good, you'd stop—" He drew her into his arms, lifting her into his lap. "You'd stop thinkin', stop worryin', stop—"

"I should warn you, Tate, I'm not very good at this."

"Good at what?" He knew damn well what, but he was going to make her say it. Here she was, cuddled against him like a kitten, and she was taking that instructive tone with him again, the one she used to protect herself. He'd always been a threat to her somehow, and, as always, she was trying to keep one foot on the floor, just in case she decided to run. Well, he wasn't about to *let* her run. Not tonight.

"I'm not the best lover." She drew a shaky breath. Tate wondered when and how she'd arrived at that conclusion. "I want to be good at it, but I know I'm not."

She just knew, and that was that. The rest he would have to figure out for himself.

"I am." He lifted her hair and traced the delicate arch of her ear with the tip of his tongue. "You want me to show you how?"

"I don't know." She shivered when he blazed a damp trail down her neck. "You probably think this is a funny conversation to be having with a woman who's somehow managed to produce two children."

"You hear me laughin'?"

"No. I appreciate that." She slipped her arms around him, shifting in his lap. "Is there room for me here? With you?"

"If we stick close together." He slid his hands up and down her back, teasing himself with the feel of soft flannel and the knowledge that there was nothing beneath it but Amy. "Is it still too soon? I know how to make love to you, Amy, but there are some things about a woman's body that are still a mystery to me."

"You've seen me at my... well, my least appealing."

She couldn't stand the idea of coming apart in front of anyone.

Oh, Amy. Her struggle with words and images touched him almost as deeply as her struggle with pain. "Why do you think of it that way? Because I was there?"

"No. I guess I shouldn't think of it at all." She pressed her face against his neck and kissed him there. "I guess I'm afraid it might bother you, and I'm afraid I'm not pretty enough or sexy enough or—"

"You trusted me then because you had to." He slid back, cradling her, entreating her as he took her into bed with him. "Trust me now because you want to. Let me decide how beautiful you are."

He peppered her face with kisses while he unbuttoned her nightgown. "I want to kiss your breasts," he whispered, sliding down into position. "I'll be gentle."

He laved each one carefully, nuzzling, kissing, making them tighten. He could feel the passion rising in her, but he knew from the tension he felt in her body that she struggled still. Her instinct was to hold back. "I taste milk," he said.

"I'm sorry. I can't—"

"Don't keep it from me." He swirled his tongue over her peak, relishing it like an ice-cream cone. "Amy's milk. It's the only kind I like."

"Oh, Tate, you'll make me..."

"Does it feel good?"

"It makes me want..."

"Good." He kissed the valley between her breasts. She buried her fingers in his hair and held him while she gulped deep breaths, struggling to regain control.

He wasn't going to give it to her. He knew damn well it was the last thing she needed right now. She needed to *lose* control, and by damn, he was just the man. He was *just* the man. He whisked her nightgown over her head and slid down more, licking a stray drop of milk as he kissed the underside of one breast. "Do they hurt?" he asked. "Are they too full?"

"No, I just fed... but all you have to do is..."

"Shh, don't worry about that." He kissed her, sharing the sticky sweetness that clung to his lips.

"Just tell me if anything hurts you. I'd cut off my arm before I'd hurt you, sweetheart, so just tell me."

"Your arm?"

Okay, so the protrusion straining against her thigh wasn't an arm, but he wasn't going to hurt her with it, either. Damn, she was teasing him. She touched her lips to his forehead, and in the dark he could feel the curve of her smile. "You don't get to laugh, either, woman." He slid his hand over her belly and kneaded gently, the way he had weeks ago. "Is it back to its normal size?" he wondered.

"I think it's—" She caught her breath as he caressed her, his hand nearly bridging the span of her pelvic cradle. "I'm flabby there," she said, but her soft groan told him that she was also aroused there. And lower. He sensed that the tension inside her was drifting lower, and he chased it with a slow hand. He didn't have to hurry. He knew where it was going, and he knew he would catch up.

He kissed her tenderly and hungrily, supplicating and demanding, and gaining wondrous kisses in return. He was gaining on her. "Relax for me, sweetheart."

Ah, her thighs were strong and stubborn, but her need was growing stronger. His tongue stroked hers, while down below he explored her springing hair, her damp folds, her soft, warm secrets. Deep in his loins he throbbed like a swollen thumb, but he knew what Amy's body had endured, and self-restraint was within his power. "Tell me when we have to stop."

With a delicate touch he stroked her until she responded urgently, pressing herself against his hand, inviting a deeper touch. "Don't stop," she pleaded. "Oh, Tate, don't stop."

He hovered over her, brushed her hair back from her face and kissed her. He was fully prepared to make the magic just for her, but he wasn't prepared for her quick gasp when he tried to slide his finger deeper. "Oh, sweetheart, I'm hurting you." He withdrew, stroking her thighs in the hope of comforting her.

"No, it's okay. I'm okay, Tate. My checkup... I'm—"

"Shh, you're not ready." He wasn't sure where it had come from, but he kissed away the dampness on her cheeks.

She groaned, running her hands up his back, digging her blunt nails in when she reached his shoulders. "That's for me to decide," she said huskily. "It might have to hurt a little."

"I can go as slow as you want."

"How about as fast as I want?"

"That, too. But if I hurt you inside, you tell me, okay?" As he spoke, he reached into the drawer in the nightstand and withdrew a foil packet. "You don't have to be strong for me, Amy. If I can't give you pleasure now, I won't—"

"I can't get pregnant now, Tate. At least, I *probably*—"

He smiled, palming the packet as he smoothed his thumb over her forehead, hoping to banish all probably-nots. "This doesn't sound like my cautious little Black-Eyed Susan."

"I told you I wasn't very good at this." She slid one tentative hand over his hard buttock. "But I want to be. I want to be...memorable for you."

He would never forget her shy, gentle hand on his hip. "Keep touching me, and I'll remember."

She did, and he returned the favor. He caressed her until she lost the last vestige of tight control and quivered in his hand, entrusting him with a rare moment of complete vulnerability. She was eager for him now, open to him with no reservations, no limitations, save the one he willingly placed on himself for her protection. She greeted his penetration with a soft, welcoming sound.

He groaned with the pleasure of immersing himself fully in her warm passage. "Put your hands on my chest," he implored. "Feel my heart beating and touch my..." His own nipples were sensitive, as she discovered with her fingertips. "Mmm, that's good. You can talk to me, Amy."

"I don't want to sound—oooooh, Tate."

"I want you to sound 'oh, Tate.' I'll remember every soft, sweet word."

"I'm afraid to talk," she whispered as she rolled her hips to meet the thrust of his. "This feels too good."

"Ain't that the..." The truth, which was ecstasy, which was bearing down upon him faster and without regard for... "Come with me, Amy."

She drew a quick breath, coming apart, shattering deliciously in his arms. "Stay with me, Tate."

"Like this, yes," he crooned close to her ear as he drew her knees up to his waist. "Let me take you with me."

She clamped her legs around him as she arched and lifted, unfurled and set sail.

Neither could move at first, and when they stirred, it was like a dance in slow motion. They nestled together, eyes closed, hands languidly touching damp skin, ears hearing the soft whistle of cold winds and hearts content in the shelter of a loving embrace.

"You okay?" he asked finally.

She nodded, and then in a small voice asked, "You?"

"Oh, yeah."

Over in the corner, one of the dogs yawned.

"Who asked you?" Tate's chuckle rumbled deep in his chest. "I'd have to say this is the best I've been in I don't know how long."

"That's for me to say, isn't it?"

"Pardon me." He traced his finger along the top of her shoulder before he kissed it. "Was I okay?"

"Best I've ever—" she pressed her face against his neck and whispered "—*had,* and I know I shouldn't say that."

"Give it a rest, honey." He caught himself and groaned. "I didn't mean 'honey.' I meant—" he kissed her again "—for both of us to give it a rest. This whole routine between us. Just give it a rest and let ourselves be together the way we've both been dreamin' about lately." He brushed his lips across her forehead. "Haven't we? I know I have."

"And now you know I have. And I shouldn't." He groaned, and she stretched her arm around him, hugging him close. "I'm not regretting anything, except . . . Well, just look what happened tonight. Jody got out of the house without my knowledge. Where was my head?"

"Were you thinking about me? Were you thinkin' that the weather was bad, and I'd been outside for quite a while, freezin' my—"

"—tail off, I know. It's a nice one, too." She reached down and patted one rock-hard cheek. "Yes, I was thinking about you, hoping you were all right, wondering any one of the many things I've been wondering about you."

"Satisfy any of that curiosity tonight?"

"Satisfied . . . something. Not the questions, but—"

"The woman." Thank God. He'd been a little worried at first. "That's good. You're more woman than anyone I've ever known, my pretty Black-Eyed Susan, and you're a challenge and a half."

"Really," she said lightly. "I don't know who you're comparing me to, but when I said 'the best I've had—'" She huddled against him, as if she wanted him to hide her from something. "I didn't mean it the way it sounded."

"It didn't sound any *way*. I knew what you meant." He turned her in his arms, belly to belly, knees to knees. "You need a man, Amy. There's no shame in that."

"Then why does it sound so . . . shameful?"

"Maybe because—" he kissed the soft swell of her breast, and she sighed "—you know I'm the man you need."

She groped for a denial, but none would come when he touched her breast as reverently as he did. Silence, followed by soft, mingled breaths and appreciative sighs, spoke of sweet accord. He claimed his point with a kiss.

Chapter Ten

As quickly as it had come, the Montana blizzard blew across the Dakota plains to become a Minnesota blizzard, leaving drifts of snow glistening in the morning sun. Jody had already forgotten the terror of blowing snow sweeping him across the yard on Christmas night. Snow pillows were friendlier, and he was ready to play in them. Amy bundled him up in his snowsuit and sent the dogs outside with him. "Stay right in the yard," she warned.

"I'm going to make a snow castle."

"I want to be able to see it from the window, okay?"

She later took her coffee into the living room, tapped on the window and waved. Jody waved back and pointed his mittened hand at the snow angel he'd just made. Then he waved again, and Amy turned to find Tate standing just behind her, waving back.

"You certainly move quietly," she said.

"Not as quietly as you do." The smile in his eyes said they shared some new secrets. "Did you find the quarters a little cramped last night?"

She glanced back out the window. New secrets posed new problems for her this morning.

"I didn't expect you to stay," he said quietly. "Just wanted you to know I missed you."

"I don't want Jody to think..." She kept her eyes on what was going on outside the window. Her child was playing with his plastic snow-block maker, thinking only that his mother and his new cowboy idol were inside watching him. "Obviously, he knows that moms and dads sleep in the same bed. I don't want to confuse him with other... ideas."

"You're still a good mother, Amy. A good woman." Tate stepped up close behind her and laid his hands on her shoulders. "What happened last night didn't change that."

She closed her eyes, allowing the light, woodsy scent of his after-shave to fill her head with erotic images of the night before, but only briefly. It was as risky an indulgence as enjoying the feel of his strong hands. She opened her eyes wide and trained them on her busy little boy as she gripped the warm stoneware mug in both hands. "You mean, what happened last night with Jody?" she asked tightly.

"You know what I mean." He leaned close to her ear, his chin brushing the thick braid that lay over one shoulder. "I mean, what happened with me."

"I went looking for it, didn't I?" Her voice went a little hoarse. She cleared her throat, determined to be nothing more than matter-of-fact. "I asked for it."

"*It?*"

"You." She set her coffee on the lamp table and turned to look him in the eye. "I went looking for you, Tate. I wanted *you.*"

It galled her that the confession clearly pleased him. He tried to take her in his arms, and she saw the confusion she caused him when she stepped out of his reach. She bolstered her resolve by telling herself that he was taking certain things for granted after just one night. He didn't understand her situation at all. Just like a man.

"I've decided to sell out, come spring."

He stared, confounded by the news. "When did you make that decision?"

"To sell out?" She shrugged, turning to the window again. "It's always been one of the options under consideration. Lately I've had to think about it more seriously. I have two small children. It's foolish for me to think I can give them the attention they need while I'm trying to run a business that demands..." She spared him a glance. "Well, you know what it demands."

"A lot of work. You need help." *You need me, Amy.*

"Hired help isn't always reliable." *But I do need you, Tate.* "If I can get through lambing, I'll make some money. My herd will be worth more with the lambs on the ground. But I need to know—" Watching Jody arrange a row of snow blocks gave her time to swallow some pride. *I need you, but how long can I count on you?* "How long can you stay, Tate?"

Now he was watching Jody, too, and his answer came without emotion. "I told you I'd get you through the winter."

"Last night complicated things, didn't it?"

"How so?" He gave a mirthless chuckle. "You think I'm gonna require more than room and board?"

"You didn't require anything." She faced him. "I was the one."

"Amy—"

"I want to pay you, Tate." She *had* to pay him. She knew it wouldn't keep him there any longer than this whim of his lasted, but it was the only way she could make peace with the way she felt about their tenuous arrangement. He was doing her too damn many favors.

"For what?" he demanded.

"For all that you've done."

"I've done what you needed me to do."

"Yes." She folded her arms, hugging herself tightly. "More than you bargained for. More than you hired yourself out to—"

"Stop it!" he growled. "Why can't you just ask me?" He closed his hands over her shoulders and recited the words carefully, as though she might be hard of hearing. "'I need you, Tate.' Is that so hard to say?"

She lifted her chin and turned her face away. One, two deep breaths helped her fight back the tears that threatened to betray her. She'd admitted to the mistake of wanting him, but *wanting* was different. With the exception of an occasional human indulgence, she routinely did without many of the things she wanted. Wanting could be kept under control, but needs had to be met. The children's needs, her own needs—it was up to Amy to provide for those. It always had been.

"Ken left some good horses," she told Tate in her most controlled, informative tone. "All registered stock, but they're not saddle-broke. I know horse prices aren't great right now, but I want you to take your pick. For every month that you've been here, every month that you stay, I want you to have one of those horses."

"What kind of services are you trying to pay me for, Amy?"

She pressed her lips together firmly. She wouldn't let his anger scare her. She could feel the power in the hands that gripped her shoulders, but she could also feel his restraint. He couldn't intimidate her. No man could. He could leave today if he wanted to, and she would get along fine without him.

"I'll stay. I told you that." He released her, his arms dropping heavily to his sides. "I'll stay and do what needs doing. Herd your sheep, deliver your baby, have a talk with your son—whatever."

She stared, startled by the knowledge that deep down she believed in his promise.

"Oh, yeah, and I can also take you to bed and give you the best damn lovin' you've ever had." He quirked a cocky smile. "Jack-of-all-trades, that's me. All that for a few broom tails?"

She affected a careless shrug. "It's all I can come up with right now."

"Well, I ain't that cheap, lady. I'm gonna cost you dearly."

"The wages of sin, I suppose."

"What sin? You mean what I got last night? Was that supposed to be my wages and your sin?" He took advantage of the momentary paralysis of her tongue. "Or was it the other way around? Damn, you've got me confused."

"I don't want to take advantage of you," she said tightly.

"Likewise," he assured her with a smug grin. "So I'm not about to take my wages out in trade. You'll have to come up with something better."

"I wasn't *offering* to pay for your..." She was tempted to put a bag over that grin. "I need your help, Tate," she said, forcing an even tone, "and I'm not suggesting anything—" *Stop that aggravating nodding.* "—unseemly. I'm only trying to—"

"That's a start. 'I need your *help*, Tate.'" He was on his way out of the room, wagging his finger and being a damn smart aleck as he went. "I like the sound of that. That's gettin' there."

"Where are you going?"

"The baby's cryin'." He paused. At first it was quiet, but then came the muffled squall. Tate's tone mimicked her at her most indulgently instructive. "I'm going to pick her up. And if I had the equipment," he said, hands on his T-shirt-clad chest, "I'd feed her, too. But even a jack-of-all-trades has his limits."

*   *   *

He knew she didn't want to need him. Needing his *help* was difficult enough for Amy, but needing *him*— needing Tate Harrison—was like having the flu. She figured she would get over it. And maybe she would. If she did, hell, he'd never really pictured himself being tied down, especially not to a bunch of sheep and a piece of ground just outside Overo, Montana, and halfway to nowhere.

The Christmas blizzard gave way to a January thaw, and Tate used the respite to his advantage. He built the slatted barn door he'd mentally devised before Amy had declared her intention to sell out. His design allowed for a choice of doors. Amy was impressed. She also liked his wall-mounted hayracks and grain feeders, which he modestly claimed were "real easy to knock together." She was less excited when he rigged up a corral, using portable steel fence panels, and began breaking horses.

He figured he could have at least four or five greenbroke by spring thaw. He didn't have time to make good saddle horses out of them, but some of them had potential. He enjoyed lecturing Jody on the subject, pointing out each animal's strengths and weaknesses, from conformation to temperament. He predicted which ones would really be worth something when Amy decided to sell them and lamented the fact that they would be worth even more if he had more time to work with them. The summer, maybe.

Given the chance, Jody would make a good horseman someday, if Amy would ever ease up on the rules. He had to stay off the fence, stay in the pickup, stay away from the horses when Tate wasn't around, stay away from the hooves, stay away from the teeth, and on and on. To her credit, Amy never said, "Your dad was killed by a horse," but her distress was apparent every time she came out to the corral when Tate was working the horses. And it annoyed the hell out of him every time she called Jody into the house because he'd been "bothering Tate long enough."

"Nobody in this house bothers me except you," he told her privately when she came out to the corral one day. "And you bother me plenty."

"Nobody's got you tied to the hitching post, cowboy. You can mosey on anytime."

"Cute." He watched the boy and his trusty stickhorse disappear into the toolshed, where he'd been sent to fetch a leather punch. "Are you trying to keep Jody away from me?"

"Of course not. He loves you like a brother."

"Brother?" He felt slighted, and feeling slighted made him feel mean. He gave her a mean-spirited smile. "What's the matter with *uncle?* You don't like that word?"

"Big brothers eventually move on, and they never realize how much little brothers miss them."

"Yeah, well, Kenny was like a brother to me, so the analogy doesn't quite work."

Jody appeared in the doorway of the toolshed. He waved the leather punch in the air, and Tate nodded his approval.

"You're right about one thing, though," Tate confided absently. He was pleased to see that Jody wasn't forgetting to close the door, and that he was carrying the tool back at a sedate walk, exactly as instructed. "The boy loves me. Unconditionally, no questions asked. And I love him right back the same way." He adjusted his hat as he looked Amy in the eye. "Believe it or not, I am capable of that. I don't care whose kid he is, I love him like my own."

She believed him. Now that she knew he was capable of giving more of himself than she'd ever thought possible, her heart ached all the more with the need to ask for another little piece of him for herself. But she was too proud. He'd been spending more of his evenings in town lately, which she regarded as a warm-up activity for a man with itchy feet. She tried not to lie awake and listen for the sound of his pickup. When she heard it, she tried not to notice what numbers were illuminated on her bedside clock. And when she didn't hear it, she tried not to imagine what or who might be keeping him out so late.

The month of February was torn off the Overo Farm and Ranch Co-Op calendar, and March came in with a lamb.

"We've got a baby comin'," Tate announced from the back door as he pulled off his work gloves.

"Already?" Amy pulled the plug on the dishwater and reached for a hen-and-chick print towel. "You're sure?"

"I suspect the signs are about the same for a ewe as they are for a cow or a mare." Tate tipped his hat back and grinned. "Human females like to keep you guessin', but you take their clothes off, the signs are probably pretty much the same."

"That's true. That's absolutely true." From the look in his eye, she could have sworn he was just as excited about the prospect of lambing as she was. Maybe he was the wolf at her door. "Your lunch is ready."

Tate's news seemed to wake up the house. Jody turned off the Saturday-morning cartoons, and Karen called from her crib. But Amy had to hurry out to the barn and see for herself what was going on. She'd counted the days and figured on almost another week before lambing would start. Now she would have to count on Tate, who was helping himself to a cup of coffee, and Jody, who was slurping up a bowl of cereal. They would have to spell her from a few duties while she did the job she felt called to do.

"You'll change your mind about sheep when you see the lambs, Tate. They're just as cute as—" She put Karen in his arms and smiled when the baby grabbed his chin. "Well, not as cute as *human* babies, but cuter than calves. I forgot to tell you about the lambing pens."

"I found them," he said. "I've already got a couple set up, and as soon as I have a cup of coffee..." He smiled down at Karen, who was trying to examine his teeth. "A cup of coffee and a couple of little baby fingers..."

"Lambing is my job."

With a glance he questioned her good sense.

"Your hands are too big, Tate." To emphasize the contrast, she put her hand over the back of his just as Karen laid claim to his thumb.

"Hey, that looks like Papa Bear, Mama Bear and Baby Bear," Jody managed to announce despite a mouth full of milk.

The look in Tate's eyes softened as one dilemma crowded out another. Amy nodded, smiling wistfully. "Mine are just the right size, you see. I have to help my mamas get their babies born. That much I owe them."

Tate had been party to many a calving, but delivering Karen had changed his outlook on the miracle of birth. Amy was right about the lambs. Those little wobbly-legged woollies were irresistible. Her skill and patience as a midwife were remarkable. Tate was content to observe the process while he tended the children. Some of the ewes required Amy's help in delivery, which often meant slipping a deft hand into the birth canal to assist a lamb in making its debut.

Most of the ewes produced twins, and one even had healthy triplets. Amy determined that the runt of the three would have to be bottle-fed. The death of three young ewes left orphans, two of which were successfully "grafted" on to ewes that had lost their lambs. Amy wrapped the pelts of the dead lambs around the orphans so that the adoptive mothers would accept them as their own. She graciously accepted Tate's offer to do the skinning.

That left two lambs to become "bottle babies," which pleased Jody immensely. Amy confided that raising orphans on the bottle was never profitable, and most sheep men didn't bother. "Sheep *women*," she said, "are different. When we sell the herd, we'll be keeping those bottle babies."

They were different, all right, Tate thought. She tried to talk offhandedly about selling her sheep, and she probably could have fooled almost anybody else. But Tate saw the pain in her eyes. Once lambing was over, she would use up what feed she had, and then she would put the herd on the market. Before the fields were lush with grass, she would sell out. She wouldn't have to worry about predators this year, she declared with artificial cheer. And shearing would be someone else's problem.

Leaving Amy and the kids would be Tate's problem. The more she mused about making her own preparations, the less he had to say about anything at all. The ground had thawed, and the first pale blooms of camas and sego lilies were beginning to dot the hillsides among the first green spikes of new grass. If he were planning to graze the livestock, he would take note of the poisonous camas and keep the animals away from them. He would be looking for coyotes, and he would be thinking about replacing a couple of sections of fence with the lamb creeps he'd been building. He'd modeled them after a picture he'd found in one of Amy's sheep-raising books. Not that he'd *read* it; he'd just sort of flipped through the pages. And not that he was thinking seriously about *any* of this stuff. A grazing plan had just sort of crossed his mind.

When he ran into Marianne and Patsy at the bar one night, he quietly took exception to a comment Marianne made about his "cozy little arrangement with

Amy." But he wasn't about to tell the women that Amy was talking about selling out. Marianne would have been on the phone with her lawyer in a New York minute, trying to find out how soon she could get her damn core samples taken. Not that he cared about a few holes punched in the pasture, but Marianne's claim that there was money lurking below ground didn't impress him much, either. If they found anything, it was likely to be coal. And he had to agree with Amy about strip mining. It wasn't a pretty sight.

Faced with Amy's quandary, he'd forgotten all about his own plans to sell his land. When Marianne brought that issue up, he paid for his drink and called it a night. He wasn't sure why he was grinding his back teeth as he left the bar. Probably had something to do with the smell of Patsy's perfume.

It was almost midnight, but the kitchen light was still on, and Amy was still up. She was sitting at the table paging through a magazine, a steaming cup of tea close at hand. If he didn't know any better, he would think she wasn't planning to be up at her usual predawn hour.

"Waiting up for me?" He was trying for a touch of sarcasm, but it just wasn't there. He liked the idea too damn much to make light of it.

"The baby's been fussy."

"Seems pretty quiet to me." Little Karen had been sleeping through the night for weeks now.

"Would you like some coffee?"

"No, thanks. I'm sober enough." He tossed his denim jacket over a hook, thinking that if he couldn't work up any sarcasm, maybe he could bait her just a little. "You've got no business waiting up for me, Amy. What I do is my business."

"I wasn't waiting up for you. But you're early."

"Compared to what?" He pulled out the chair across from her, spun it around and straddled it, folding his arms over the back. "Compared to last week? Last month?" She glanced up from her magazine. "Compared to when Kenny used to come home?"

"Kenny always came home." She gave him a pointed look—though what her point was, he wasn't sure—then turned a page and found something that seemed to interest her more than he did. She tore into a corner of the page as she rattled on. "Ken had his faults and his weaknesses, but he gave us a home, and he was part of it. Always."

"Good for him." She glanced up, and he nodded. "I mean that. He inherited this place. Big deal. The truth is, *you* were good for *him*. How good was *he,* Amy?" Her eyes betrayed nothing as she carefully laid the coupon aside. "How good was he for *you?*" Tate demanded quietly.

"I don't see how his best friend could ask a question like that." She turned another page. "He gave me two children."

"*I* was here the night Karen was born," Tate reminded her. Her hand went still, the page stalled at an angle. "I was with you that night. She came—" Amy looked into his eyes as he gestured poignantly "—from your body into my hands. I've never felt so..."

"So... what?" she asked, as mesmerized by the memory as he was.

"Yeah, so what." He stood abruptly and jammed his hands into his front pockets, bursting the bubble with a shrug. "I shouldn't have said 'big deal.' I didn't mean to knock Kenny or anything the two of you... had. Okay?"

"I think you misunderstood, Tate. I meant..." But he was done. He was getting his jacket back off the hook. "Where are you going?" she asked.

Back to the Jackalope, he should have said, but her question had sounded sufficiently meek to warrant an honest response. "Out to the barn." Downstairs first, for something to keep him warm. Maybe blankets would be enough. "I need to take care of some things before I turn in."

She should just leave him alone, she told herself as she headed across the yard. He hadn't been out there very long, and he was probably having a cigarette. It was a clear, crisp night. Nice night to be outside. She visited Daisy and Duke in their kennel, then told herself to go back into the house. But herself wasn't listening very well. The light was still on in the barn. She pushed the side door open.

"Tate?"

"Up here." She saw his black cowboy hat first, then his face, then his denim collar turned up to his jawline. He peered down from the loft. "What's up? Kids okay?"

"They're fine. They're sound asleep." As she closed the door behind her, she noticed a pair of green feline eyes peeking down from the loft, too. "What are you doing?"

"I had a crazy yen to sleep out here tonight."

"In the barn?"

"Ol' Cinnamon Toast has been up here cleaning out the mice, and I just mucked out the pens today. Put down fresh straw." He flipped open a green wool blanket. "It's aboveground, which is a real plus. I feel like campin' out tonight." The hat disappeared, and there was some rustling of hay. "Could you hit the light on your way out?"

When the light went out, it was pitch-dark for a moment, but then her eyes adjusted to the dimmer light emitted through the clerestory windows directly across from the loft. The moonlight would be nice, she thought. It would flood across his makeshift bed like stardust. She climbed the steps quietly, although she knew he heard her coming.

"Tate? You'll get cold out here."

"If I do, I know where the house is."

She climbed over the top of the ladder and stood at the foot of the pallet he'd made. He'd pulled the blanket up to his chest, pillowed his neck in his hands and covered his face with his cowboy hat. His boots stuck out at the end of the blanket. He looked incredibly long. And he was ignoring her.

Amy cleared her throat. "As long as you've declared a truce, maybe we could..."

"Have ourselves a roll in the hay?"

"Have a talk about...the best way to go about selling the livestock." She knelt on the corner of the pallet. "I'll need your help, but I don't want you to think you have to—"

"I don't think I *have* to. Go back to the house, Amy. Give me some peace."

"It's too cold out here," she insisted. "I won't have you sleeping in the barn."

"What're you gonna do about it?"

"Well..." Good question. "I'm just going to sit here."

He shoved his hat back as he braced himself on his elbows and gave her a cool stare. "You can't control me the way you did Kenny. That's what scares you about me, isn't it?"

"Control? I couldn't control Ken. He puttered around with his horses and talked about all the things he was going to do around here, but I couldn't get him to make a *real* decision about anything important to—" her hands flopped against her knees in frustration "—to save his life."

"Kenny was my friend. He was a good-hearted guy, and we had some good times together. But he never took charge of anything." He sat up, leaned across his own knees and reached for her hand. "A woman wants a man to take charge once in a while, doesn't she?"

"Yes, but not—"

"Not to push her around." He tugged on her hand, cautiously reeling her into his bed. "Not to take her security away, but just to say, 'Lean on me for a while.'"

"That would be nice."

"Damn right." He lifted the edge of the top blanket and drew her underneath it. "So I'm gonna show you just how a man takes charge."

There was no more talk of selling anything. There was very little talk at all, and when they spoke, it was only of what was happening between them at the moment. They didn't undress completely. Instead they delighted in undoing buttons, one at a time, and finding places that needed kissing. Each piece of clothing became an envelope to be expertly unsealed, the contents to be secretly investigated without being removed. They were like first lovers, exploring one another, sharing secrets in a secret place. They teased one another about wanting to get into each other's pants, tortured each other by dragging zippers down and touching warm skin with cool hands. Inevitably the torture became exquisitely sensuous as hands and lips sought the deeper secrets nestled in the wedge-shaped envelopes of open zippers.

He had not hoped to love her this way again. Reckless as he was, he had never been the right man, but he would do for now. And for now, he would do well.

She had not expected to be held and touched this way again. Sensible as she was, she always sought moderation, but not tonight. Tonight she abandoned caution and demanded no compromise. Tonight his way was better.

Tonight she whispered love words while she suckled him. Tonight she made him moan as relentlessly as he did her. They kissed and touched with feverish abandon. He called her *honey,* because, he said, she tasted like honey. "And I've never said that to anyone before."

He was, she told him, a man for all seasons and all times of the day, but especially beautiful in the moonlight. Her hands cherished his every contour. "Like polished marble all over, all over, all over."

"We're going to shoot the moon," he promised as he eased himself inside her. It took some ardent stroking, some rhythmic pumping and some zealous writhing, but they did. They not only shot the moon, they made a whole new crater.

"Don't go yet," he said when she'd recovered strength enough to move. "Stay with me a little longer."

"We should go inside. We could…" She wanted to take him to her bed, but Jody might find him there. His room was right across the hall. Amy's good judgment put her wanting in its place.

And Tate didn't need any diagrams. "We'd have to get dressed," he lamented as he cradled her against his chest. "I'd have to fasten this." He couldn't locate a bra cup without brushing the back of his hand across her nipple. "And then I couldn't do this anymore." He smiled when he'd coaxed her nipple into a bead.

"You're a tricky one, Tate Harrison," she whispered contentedly.

He tongued her nipple gently, just one more time. Just for good measure. "How long will you nurse Karen?"

She answered with a soft groan.

He tightened his arms around her hips, holding her to him as he pressed his face between her breasts. "Who gets weaned first, her or me?"

Like his lovemaking, his teasing hurt sometimes, but she could hide the hurt as long as he couldn't see her face. She tunneled her fingers into his hair and held him, his ear a scant inch from her thrumming heart. "Whoever grows up first, I guess."

Chapter Eleven

He woke up shivering in his blankets, and Amy was gone. Responsible Amy. She had children to look after—thank God she was responsible. He would have kept her up in that loft, rolling in his arms, halfway into summer. A loft was much better than a pumpkin shell, not that he owned either one. But he had a pickup, a passbook savings account and a piece of Montana ground. He was worth *something,* anyway. If the woman couldn't see that, it was time to point it out to her. The sun would be up soon. He decided that sunrise would be a damn good time.

He showered and shaved, and while he was getting himself dressed in the shirt she'd made for him, he could hear activity overhead. Karen was making those cute little baby noises. She was just naturally an early bird, but it was unusual for Jody to be clomping around the kitchen in his prized cowboy boots at this hour.

They were all outside by the time he got upstairs. He could see them through the front window, Karen all bundled up in her stroller and Jody standing out there hipshot like a cool cowhand, leaning on his broomstick horse as if it were the gatepost on the approach to a ten-thousand-acre spread. Amy was dragging something out of the back of her pickup, which she'd backed up to the edge of the yard. Early-morning light brightened the sky all around them. The lavender hills sloped in silhouette against the pale yellow dawn.

Tate grabbed his hat and headed out the back, slamming the storm door shut behind him. Amy looked up and smiled. "We were just about to go looking for you. We're planting Karen's tree."

"You're gonna plant a tree just before you move out?"

"Whether we're moving or not, these things have to be done in their season, and it's the season for tree planting." She hooked a stray lock of hair behind her ear and pointed across the yard. "Jody's tree is that paper birch. See how nice and tall it's growing?"

Jody trotted across the yard to reacquaint himself with his birch tree. "It's budding, too," he boasted.

"We thought Karen's should be a Christmas tree." Tate took over the job of unloading the young nursery-raised blue spruce from the back of the pickup. "I don't want to block the view from the window, though," Amy mused as she surveyed the yard.

She wore an old yellow sweatshirt and faded blue jeans, and she looked as fresh and naturally pretty as the morning sky. She caught him staring at her, though, so he had to tear his eyes away and give some serious consideration to the problem at hand.

"I've been thinkin' we needed a windbreak over there by your garden." He quirked her a questioning brow, and she nodded. He carried the tree and pushed the stroller. Jody and Outlaw, Jr., galloped along behind, while Amy donned her gardening gloves and brought up the rear. She carried the shovel.

Jody cut a wide circle around his sister's stroller. "Remember when we went out and got the Christmas tree, Tate?"

"I remember." Along with Christmas trees past, he thought. Trees had a way of making nice memories. He set the tree down close to where he wanted to see it take root, then he turned, eyeing the shovel. "You gonna let me do the digging on this project?"

"If you want to."

He took the shovel from Amy's hands and stabbed the ground with its point. He could feel her watching him with those earth-mother eyes of hers. When she was satisfied that he could handle the job, she dashed into the house and came back with a bucket of water and a plastic sack.

"Does that look big enough?" He knew it was plenty big, but he wanted to make sure she was satisfied with his work. This was one morning he wasn't giving her anything to complain about.

"It looks perfect." She knelt beside the tree and started tapping the pot to loosen the roots.

"Here, let me help." Tate hunkered down beside her and took the plastic pot in his big hands, breaking it down the side. Then he took out his jackknife. "The tool-of-all-trades for the jack-of-all-trades." He was really going to impress her now. He'd had a seasonal job with the Forest Service years ago. He knew that a competent planter of trees always scored the root ball.

The sun appeared in a crotch in the foothills, spilling fruit-basket colors across the sky as Tate lifted Karen from the stroller. They all gathered around Tate's hole in the earth and watched Amy empty the contents of the plastic zipper bag. There was nothing unbeautiful about the blood from Amy's body, the tissue that had nourished her unborn baby. Tate held the tree steady with one hand. With the other he raked black loam into the hole. Other fingers plunged to his aid—Amy's slender ones, Jody's short ones and Karen's chubby ones. They pounded the first layer down, added water, and dug in again.

"Who's going to tend it?" Tate asked after the job was done.

"God takes care of the trees," Jody reported confidently. "Doesn't He, Mom?"

"The trees and the sparrows." Amy squinted against the sun's glare as she looked up at Tate. "Who's tending yours?" He looked at her questioningly. "The ones along the driveway that used to lead to your old house. There's a huge clump of daylilies that blooms there every summer. Did your mother plant those?"

"Probably." He remembered his mother's daylilies and her hollyhocks. He'd had to weed them every damn spring when she was alive. "They're still there?"

"Like Jody said, God takes care of them." She shifted Karen from one hip to the other and started toward the house. "Besides, you can't even get rid of daylilies with an eight-bottom plow."

Jody fed his orphan lambs with a huge plastic baby bottle. Amy and Tate sat side by side on the back step and watched them romp around the yard together. From their backyard kennel, Daisy and Duke let it be known that they were ready to romp, too. The lambs ignored the barking. They listened only to Jody, the voice of the milk supply.

"When Jody goes to school, he'll have two lambs on his tail," Tate said with a bemused smile. "Think that'll make the children laugh and play?"

Amy laughed as she bounced Karen on her knees. "You've been eavesdropping on the bedtime reading again."

"Karen and me both, right, sweetie?" He chucked the baby under her chin. "One night last week I walked the floor with her a little bit, and Jody's door was open just a crack. We didn't wanna interrupt, but we heard something about little lambs, and we were just curious."

"Tate, about last night . . ."

"You let me say something about last night, okay?" He detected an unusual timidity in the look she slid him. "Short and sweet."

"Yes," she said quietly. "Short, but very, very sweet."

He whispered in her ear, "I kept it up as long as I could, boss lady," and she closed her eyes and smiled. "I meant that my say will be short and sweet. *Maybe.*" She glanced up, and he chuckled. "Why is it we're always explaining what we meant after we say what we say?"

"To each other?" He nodded. She shrugged. "Maybe we don't speak the same language."

"We did last night," he recalled. The blush in her cheeks was so pretty, it stung his eyes. He had to look at something else while he said his piece. He chose Jody, tumbling in the new grass with a leggy lamb.

"I've been doin' a lot of thinking lately," Tate began cautiously. "You know, you can keep horses and sheep together real easy. They complement each other well, the way they graze. Sheep will eat plants that horses don't like, and sheep dung is good fertilizer for horse pasture. They seem like opposites, but each improves the pasture for the other."

"You have to separate them at lambing time," Amy pointed out quietly.

"So you make a few allowances." He turned to her. "You really plannin' to sell this place?"

"You really planning to sell yours?" He was ready to tell her that he wasn't sure, but she had a piece she had to say, too. "If you'd stop running long enough, you'd realize how useless all this running is. You were born to this land, Tate, this life, and it still shows, no matter how far you've tried to put it behind you."

"You wanted something different from the life you grew up with," he reminded her. "So do I. I want—"

"What?"

He smiled. "Listen to me, now. I'm trying to draw you this harmony-between-sheep-and-horses comparison."

"And I want you to tell me straight-out," she insisted. "What are you looking for, Tate?"

"I want a home and family. I want to feel like I belong, like I'm wanted and needed." He looked across the yard at Jody again. "Like somebody believes in me, trusts me. I screwed up bad once, but—"

"You were just a boy."

"I didn't know that. I thought I was supposed to be a man." He paused for a moment, thinking about that ghost and a few others. Here was an opening for him to try to put their ghosts to rest. "Kenny thought it was still okay for him to be a boy, even after he was married. He let you carry most of the load." He turned to her. "I wouldn't do that, Amy. I'm just as strong-willed as you are. We'd put it all together—what's mine with what's yours. But you'd have to be willing to share decisions with me, fifty-fifty."

She was doing her damnedest to bank up the coals on a warm smile. "Would you be wanting a few cows, too, cowboy?"

"I might. But if I can live with sheep—"

"I think I could live with cows if I had a real cowboy around," she said, too quickly, too eagerly. It was as though she'd caught herself on the verge of being happy, and it scared her, made her feel guilty. The implicit contrast was like a bucket of cold water dumped between them.

Dredging up a somber note, she glanced away. "I did love Ken."

"I know." Tate slipped his arm around her. "He was my best friend. Always." *Even when I wanted his girl for my own. Even when I wanted his wife. Even when I wanted to punch him in the face because he didn't know any better than to take the woman I wanted for granted.* "I loved him, too, Amy, but that doesn't have to come between us. He loved us. And we both did right by him."

"What you said about why we haven't always gotten along . . . Why I might have been . . . afraid of you in a way." She looked up at him again. "You might have a point."

"I might have a point." He claimed the baby, who shrieked with delight as he lifted her toward the sky in a joyful toast. "Ha-ha, I might have a *point!*"

"There's a chance we could become great compromisers," Amy said tentatively.

"We'd probably butt heads once in a while, but we'd take care of each other, too. You'd lean on me, and I'd lean on you, sort of like a jackleg fence." He was riding high now, with a pretty girl tucked under each arm. "And the kids, they'd be like the cross pieces, you know? There's a lot I could teach Jody."

"You've been like a father to him these last few months."

"I thought it was *brother.*"

"Father," she amended belatedly. "And there aren't too many fathers who can say they've actually delivered their daughters into the world."

He bounced Karen in his arm. "You remember that night, little darlin'? You popped your head into the world, and this was the first face to greet you." She patted his smooth-shaven cheek with a chubby hand. "It was a little bristly that night, as I recall."

"She was glad you were there." Amy put her arm around his waist and smiled up at him. "So was her mom."

"I know you needed me that night," he said. "How about now? Not just my help, Amy. *Me*." He needed to hear her say it. "It's not a weakness to need someone," he professed, as much for his own benefit as for hers. And suddenly, for better or for worse, he didn't mind saying, "I need you."

"For what?"

"For a companion," he offered. She wasn't buying yet. "For my partner, how's that?" Better, he could tell. "For my lover," he growled in her ear. "How's that?"

"It would be a lovely thought." She challenged him with a look. "If you loved me."

"I don't remember when I didn't love you."

Now she smiled, and the light in her silk chocolate eyes was like sunrise at sea.

"And I always will, Amy. How's *that?*"

"Is it . . . really true?"

"You know it's true."

She did. She'd known it for some time. And she'd known there would be heartache if he left her and risks if he stayed.

"I think my father loved my mother, too, in his own way. And we loved him, but . . ." Oh, God, could she keep a man like Tate happy? If she gave him a place in her heart and her home, would he find it too confining for his long, tall cowboy form and being?

She sighed. "I can be good in all the roles you named, but I'm not a good gypsy. You'd have to—"

"Settle down, I know. I'm feelin' pretty settled. I've been a pretty good hired hand, haven't I?" She nodded slowly. "Fire me."

"What?"

"I want to be your husband. I want to be a father to your children." He searched the depths of her eyes. "If you think you could love me."

"I've been afraid to love you, but I've been loving you anyway. It couldn't be helped." She lowered her head and rubbed her cheek against his shoulder. His heart swelled when she finally confessed, "I need you, Tate. If you ever left me now..."

"I would die inside." She lifted her chin, then lifted her eyes to his. He smiled. "I've been runnin' in circles, endin' up back home every time."

He dipped his head, and their lips met for a long slow kiss. Karen smacked his cheek once, but it didn't faze him. Not when he heard the catch in Amy's breath over his fancy tongue stroking.

"Oh, mush," said a voice at his knee.

Tate groaned. He opened his eyes and reluctantly broke the kiss. Amy giggled as he turned a sheepish glance Jody's way. "Mush?"

"You guys gotta get married if you're gonna be kissin' like that."

"You think we'd better?" Tate asked expectantly. Jody wrinkled his nose. "Do I have your permission to marry your mom, partner?" Tate's nod summoned Jody for an exchange between cohorts. The boy leaned in closer. "Say yes, and I'll see what I can do about a horse to go with that saddle."

Jody's pogo-stick legs sprang into action. "Yes! Whoa, can you marry her today?"

"Jody!" Amy complained buoyantly. "You probably could have bid him up. I'm certainly worth more than one horse."

"I only want one." He grabbed Tate's knee, anchoring himself for one quick, anxious inquiry. "Will you be my dad then?"

"I will if your mom stops playing hard to get and says yes."

"Can we still be partners?"

"We can always be partners." He looked into the face of the only woman he'd ever petitioned for such an agreement. "You wanna be partners, Amy?"

"Kiss her again, Tate! She'll say yes if you kiss her again."

So he did kiss her. And she did say, "Yes."

* * * * *

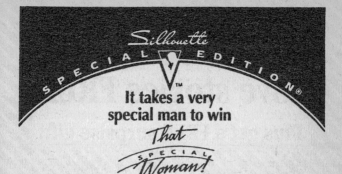

Take 4 bestselling love stories FREE

Plus get a FREE surprise gift!

HE'S AN

AMERICAN HERO

He's a cop, a fire fighter or even just a fearless drifter who gets the job done when ordinary men have given up. And you'll find one American Hero every month, only in Intimate Moments—created by some of your favorite authors. Look at what we've lined up for the last months of 1993:

October: GABLE'S LADY by Linda Turner—With a ranch to save and a teenage sister to protect, Gable Rawlings already has a handful of trouble...until hotheaded Josey O'Brian makes it an armful....

November: NIGHTSHADE by Nora Roberts—Murder and a runaway's disappearance force Colt Nightshade and Lt. Althea Grayson into an uneasy alliance....

December: LOST WARRIORS by Rachel Lee—With one war behind him, Medevac pilot Billy Joe Yuma still has the strength to fight off the affections of the one woman he can never have....

AMERICAN HEROES: Men who give all they've got for their country, their work—the women they love.

IMHER06

Silhouette SPECIAL EDITION ™®

WILD RIVER TRILOGY

by
Laurie Paige

Come meet the wild McPherson men and see how these three sexy bachelors are tamed!

In HOME FOR A WILD HEART (SE #828) you got to know Kerrigan McPherson.

In A PLACE FOR EAGLES (SE #839) Keegan McPherson got the surprise of his life.

And in THE WAY OF A MAN (SE #849, November 1993) Paul McPherson finally meets his match.

Don't miss any of these exciting titles, only for our readers—and only from Silhouette Special Edition!

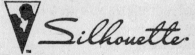

He staked his claim…

HONOR BOUND

by
New York Times
Bestselling Author

previously published under the pseudonym Erin St. Claire

As Aislinn Andrews opened her mouth to scream, a hard
hand clamped over her face and she found herself face-
to-face with Lucas Greywolf, a lean, lethal-looking
Navajo and escaped convict who swore he wouldn't hurt
her— *if* she helped him.

Look for HONOR BOUND at your favorite
retail outlet this January.

Only from…

 *Silhouette*

where passion lives. SBHB

When the only time you have for yourself is…

Christmas is such a busy time—with shopping, decorating, writing cards, trimming trees, wrapping gifts.…

When you do have a few *stolen moments* to call your own, treat yourself to a brand-new *short* novel. Relax with one of our Stocking Stuffers— or with all six!

Each STOLEN MOMENTS title is a complete and original contemporary romance that's the perfect length for the busy woman of the nineties! Especially at Christmas…

And they make perfect **stocking stuffers**, too! (For your mother, grandmother, daughters, friends, co-workers, neighbors, aunts, cousins—all the other women in your life!)

Look for the STOLEN MOMENTS display in December

STOCKING STUFFERS:

HIS MISTRESS Carrie Alexander
DANIEL'S DECEPTION Marie DeWitt
SNOW ANGEL Isolde Evans
THE FAMILY MAN Danielle Kelly
THE LONE WOLF Ellen Rogers
MONTANA CHRISTMAS Lynn Russell

HSM2

 **WORLDWIDE LIBRARY**

4-0 4-7 4-12

SILHOUETTE.... Where Passion Lives

Don't miss these Silhouette favorites by some of our most popular authors!
And now, you can receive a discount by ordering two or more titles!

Silhouette Desire®

#05751	THE MAN WITH THE MIDNIGHT EYES BJ James	$2.89	❑
#05763	THE COWBOY Cait London	$2.89	❑
#05774	TENNESSEE WALTZ Jackie Merritt	$2.89	❑
#05779	THE RANCHER AND THE RUNAWAY BRIDE Joan Johnston	$2.89	❑

Silhouette Intimate Moments®

#07417	WOLF AND THE ANGEL Kathleen Creighton	$3.29	❑
#07480	DIAMOND WILLOW Kathleen Eagle	$3.39	❑
#07486	MEMORIES OF LAURA Marilyn Pappano	$3.39	❑
#07493	QUINN EISLEY'S WAR Patricia Gardner Evans	$3.39	❑

Silhouette Shadows®

#27003	STRANGER IN THE MIST Lee Karr	$3.50	❑
#27007	FLASHBACK Terri Herrington	$3.50	❑
#27009	BREAK THE NIGHT Anne Stuart	$3.50	❑
#27012	DARK ENCHANTMENT Jane Toombs	$3.50	❑

Silhouette Special Edition®

#09754	THERE AND NOW Linda Lael Miller	$3.39	❑
#09770	FATHER: UNKNOWN Andrea Edwards	$3.39	❑
#09791	THE CAT THAT LIVED ON PARK AVENUE Tracy Sinclair	$3.39	❑
#09811	HE'S THE RICH BOY Lisa Jackson	$3.39	❑

Silhouette Romance®

#08893	LETTERS FROM HOME Toni Collins	$2.69	❑
#08915	NEW YEAR'S BABY Stella Bagwell	$2.69	❑
#08927	THE PURSUIT OF HAPPINESS Anne Peters	$2.69	❑
#08952	INSTANT FATHER Lucy Gordon	$2.75	❑

	AMOUNT	$ _____
DEDUCT:	10% DISCOUNT FOR 2+ BOOKS	$ _____
	POSTAGE & HANDLING	$ _____
	($1.00 for one book, 50¢ for each additional)	
	APPLICABLE TAXES*	$ _____
	TOTAL PAYABLE	$ _____
	(check or money order—please do not send cash)	

To order, complete this form and send it, along with a check or money order for the total above, payable to Silhouette Books, to: *In the U.S.*: 3010 Walden Avenue, P.O. Box 9077, Buffalo, NY 14269-9077; *In Canada*: P.O. Box 636, Fort Erie, Ontario, L2A 5X3.

Name: _____

Address: _____ City: _____

State/Prov.: _____ Zip/Postal Code: _____

*New York residents remit applicable sales taxes.
Canadian residents remit applicable GST and provincial taxes.

SBACK-OD

Ⅴ *Silhouette*